PUFFIN BOOKS

BIGFOOT AND THE HENDERSONS

The Hendersons' not altogether successful camping holiday ends in nightmare when they crash into a large, shadowy figure on the way home, and find an enormous and very smelly 'surprise' on their hands! Thinking him dead – and valuable – George decides to take the creature home, to Ernie's delight, Sarah's disgust and Nancy's horror!

Back home, the Hendersons discover that the huge beast is by no means dead: he's alive and well and *extremely* hungry. What's more, he's vegetarian, and proceeds to help himself to Nancy's sacred house plants and to bury her fur stoles in the garden out of respect for the dead.

It's rather awkward when your home gets taken over by such an *unusual* guest, especially when he's very messy, constantly hungry and impossibly big. But Harry takes everyone by surprise – he is clever, charming and totally irresistible. He wins the Hendersons' hearts, and when the hunters come to track him down the Hendersons are determined to save him . . .

A hilarious, endearing and unputdownable story based on the Universal/Amblin' Entertainment film *Bigfoot and the Hendersons*, produced by Richard Vane and William Dear and directed by William Dear.

Joyce Thompson was born in Washington in 1948. She has lived in New York and Boston, working for publishers and a media production group, and now lives in Portland, Oregon. She is the author of several novels.

Bigfoot and the Hendersons

A novel by
Joyce Thompson

Based on a screenplay by William Dear and William E. Martin & Ezra D. Rappaport

Puffin Books

PUFFIN BOOKS

Penguin Books Ltd, 27 Wrights Lane, London W8 5TZ (Publishing and Editorial)
and Harmondsworth, Middlesex, England (Distribution and Warehouse)
Viking Penguin Inc., 40 West 23rd Street, New York, New York 10010, USA
Penguin Books Australia Ltd, Ringwood, Victoria, Australia
Penguin Books Canada Ltd, 2801 John Street, Markham, Ontario, Canada L3R 1B4
Penguin Books (NZ) Ltd, 182–190 Wairau Road, Auckland 10, New Zealand

Bigfoot and the Hendersons
A novel by Joyce Thompson
Based on a screenplay by William Dear
and William E. Martin & Ezra D. Rappaport

First published in the USA by Berkley 1987
First published in Great Britain in Puffin Books 1987

Printed and bound in Great Britain by
Cox & Wyman Ltd, Reading
Typeset in Trump Mediaeval (Linotron 202)
by Rowland Phototypsetting Ltd
Bury St Edmunds, Suffolk

• Chapter One

Every year the Hendersons took their family vacation the last week of summer. The weather was too iffy in June, and July and August were the busiest months of the year at the sporting goods store where Mr Henderson worked. George Henderson knew more about boots, backpacks, tent flaps, Coleman stoves and the fifteen brands of insect repellent the store sold than any other employee of Seattle Sport and Game. Which was only natural, of course. He was the boss's son.

George had been the boss's son for – count 'em – twenty years, longer if he added in the summers he'd worked for his father when he was still in high school. Old George wasn't about to let young George take to the woods in peak camping season when he could be selling sleeping bags to somebody else. In fact, it was only after he'd worked for his dad for ten years and sold maybe two thousand Swiss army knives that George got to take his vacation in summer at all. He always recommended the model with the fish-hook remover and the portable toothpick.

George got the last week of August the same year his mom and dad traded their Jeep in for a motorized caravan and started spending February in Palm Springs. February was always rainy in Seattle and slow in sporting goods. When the old man finally gave him August, George and his family burned their snow shoes and bought a four-man tent. Every summer since, just before Labor Day in early September, they had headed for the woods.

Old George had always taken young George camping when he was a boy. He'd taught him to fish and hunt, to clean his catch and skin his kill. On these trips George had learned to be a sportsman, and something else besides. He'd come to see the beauty of the forest, to appreciate the uncomplicated quiet of life in the woods. As a kid, George hid a notebook and a pencil stub in the pocket of his chamois shirt and made quick little sketches of squirrels and rabbits and birds when his father wasn't looking. Now, when he took his family camping, George packed a Strathmore sketchbook and charcoal right alongside his shotgun and didn't care who knew it.

It was important to George that his children should learn to love the woods as much as he did. For ten years now, even the summer Nancy was pregnant with Ernie and nervous the whole time that the baby might come early, the Hendersons had spent the last week of August in their tent somewhere in the Mount Rainier National Forest. George saw no reason to part with tradition. When Nancy suggested gently that they might, just once, do something different on their vacation, like go to Disneyland, he was genuinely shocked.

'Why would anybody want to spend their vacation with thousands of other people? Besides, the air stinks down there in southern California.'

Sarah, who was in ninth grade at the time, looked up from her homework. 'If you ask me, dad, camping stinks.'

George looked at his daughter in alarm. 'Sarah!'

Sarah held her ground. 'It does, daddy. Nobody takes a bath for a whole week. Everybody smells like smoke and fish. Except Ernie. He smells like the dump.'

Above Sarah's head, George looked to Nancy for support. Nancy looked away. Sarah said, 'Tell him, mom.'

Nancy said, 'You tell him.'

'You promised, mom.'

'I've chickened out. Maybe next year.'

George looked from his wife to his daughter. 'Tell me what?' he said.

Sarah stared at her maths book.

'Nancy, what's going on here?'

Slowly, Nancy turned from the sink to face George. 'Nothing, really. It's just that apparently Sarah would rather not go camping this year.'

'Not *apparently*,' Sarah said. 'Definitely.'

The idea was so new and so shocking to George that all he could manage to say was, 'But . . .'

'Sasha's mom's already said I could stay with them,' Sarah informed her father.

'But . . . ,' George said.

'Besides, that way I could get a job and work all summer. I wouldn't have to stop before school started.'

'But . . . ,' said George.

'That way everybody could have a good time. Not just you and Ernie.' Sarah was moving in for the kill.

'We all have a good time,' George said. 'You like camping. Remember when you caught your first trout? You were so excited you made us keep it in the freezer for a whole year. You used to take it out and show your friends.'

'I was just a little kid then,' Sarah said.

'What do you think you are now, a senior citizen?' George said.

Sarah sat up straighter at the table. 'In three weeks I'm going to be fifteen years old. I start high school next year. High school, daddy. Nobody in high school goes camping with their family.'

This was news to George. 'Why not?' he asked.

Sarah sighed. She would have to explain the obvious. 'First of all, there's no hot water in the woods. There's no telephone. There's no cable television. No bus service. No electricity.'

'Of course not. That's what I love about camping. No distractions.'

'Exactly,' Sarah said.

George looked at his daughter. 'What do you need electricity for anyway?'

'To plug in my curling iron.'

'Oh, my God,' George said.

'And then,' Sarah went on, 'there's Ernie.'

Ernie picked just that moment to arrive home from baseball practice. His sneakers and jeans were caked with dirt. Nancy held up her palm like a school-crossing warden. 'Not in here, young man. I've just mopped the kitchen floor. Take those filthy things off before you come inside.'

Ernie retreated to the back porch and kicked off his tennis

shoes. His sweat socks were moderately clean – light grey with darker toes. He padded back into the kitchen, bound for the refrigerator. 'What's to eat?'

'Have an apple and some milk,' Nancy advised. 'Don't spoil your appetite.'

'He's spoiled my appetite,' Sarah said. 'Ernie, don't you ever wash your feet?'

Ernie bit loudly into a crisp Granny Smith. 'What's the matter with her?'

George felt a little more confident with another male in the house. 'Your sister,' he said, 'has just informed me that she'd rather not go camping with the family this summer. She'd rather stay with her friend Sasha in the hot, dirty city than spend a week in the woods with her family.'

'Yo,' Ernie said. 'All right! You're going to let her, aren't you, dad?'

In that instant George made up his mind. It was important to be firm with teenagers. They appreciated it. He'd read that somewhere. 'Absolutely not,' he said.

Sarah threw down her pencil so hard it bounced across the table and rolled down to the floor. 'Mom . . . ,' she wailed.

'Co-ordinated,' Ernie said.

Nancy surveyed her family with a sad smile. 'It's months till vacation,' she said. 'There's plenty of time to talk about this later.'

The Hendersons talked about it a lot. They talked about it the rest of the spring and most of the summer. Sarah still didn't want to go camping, and George still insisted that she had to. Nancy hated it. Usually family fights blew over fast. Usually someone gave in, or both parties compromised and peace was restored. But this was more than a skirmish. It was a war. Sarah was growing up and her father didn't want her to. That's how Nancy saw it. She didn't especially want her daughter to grow up either, but she was willing to accept it as inevitable. And George: his stubbornness worried her. In spite of his six feet four inches, in spite of his weird enthusiasm for football and hunting, he was really the gentlest of men. This wasn't like him.

Ernie loved it. His big sister, who could do no wrong, was

wrong. Dead wrong. Wrong enough to make Ernie right sometimes. Whenever he and Sarah got into a fight bad enough that their parents stepped in, Ernie brought up camping. Whenever Sarah wanted to do something that Ernie was too little to do himself, he brought up camping. Whenever Sarah was getting on his nerves, he mentioned camping. It was wonderful to have a new weapon in the brother–sister war. Of course, Ernie secretly hoped that Sarah would wear their father down. At nine, Ernie was still young enough to like the idea of having his parents all to himself. And he absolutely loved the idea of a whole week in the woods without his sister. For once he wanted her to get her own way.

Most of the spring and summer Sarah didn't think much about camping at all. It annoyed her the way Ernie brought it up all the time to get her in trouble and himself out of it. She certainly wasn't looking forward to spending a whole boring week in the wilderness while her hair turned to string, but mostly she had other things to think about. Her fifteenth birthday for one thing. Since her birthday was in May and junior high school graduation was in June, the Hendersons let her have one big party to celebrate both.

Then, as soon as school was out, Sarah got a job at Burger King. In June she was a trainee. By July the assistant manager decided she was smart and honest enough to work the cash register, so she didn't even have to wear a hairnet. The second week of August she was picked as Cashier of the Week and got her name up on the wall. Summer turned out hot after a rainy June, and Burger King was so busy that Sarah had to work every day and every weekend. By the time vacation rolled around Sarah was ready for it, even if she did have to spend it in the woods. She planned to sleep the whole time anyway.

George was, well, a little sad that summer. He didn't know why exactly, except that here he was looking at his fortieth birthday, the big four-oh, come February, and still working for his dad, still taking orders, still selling expensive toys to tenderfoots and greenhorns, guys who wouldn't know the difference between an elk and a moose if you drew them a picture.

That's what George wanted to do – draw pictures. At

twenty-four, right around the time Sarah was born, George was sure he'd be a famous artist by the time he was forty. In his daydreams he was a kind of Frederick Remington of the Pacific Northwest. The job was open. Mark Tobey had made some post-Expressionist squiggles and said they were the Pike Place Market, and Morris Graves did a nice job with birds, but no one had ever really captured the grandeur of God's Country as George believed it should be done. With each year that went by it seemed less likely he'd be the one to do it.

He didn't like to blame his father, but Old George had a lot to do with it. George was accepted at the University of Washington right out of high school, but the old man said he wasn't paying for his son to learn to colour – he should have got that out of his system in kindergarten. It was business administration, engineering school or nothing. George didn't want to be an engineer or an accountant. He went to work at the store, planning to quit as soon as he'd saved his own tuition. Then he met Nancy. They got married. Then Sarah came.

Sarah. That was another thing. At her fifteenth birthday party, with her first orchid pinned to her shoulder, she looked like one of those dolls she used to play with when she was little. What were they called? She looked just like a Barbie. And she didn't want to go camping with the family this summer. His little girl wasn't just growing up, she was growing away.

When the Henderson station wagon, packed to the gills, backed out of the driveway that August, everyone in it had mixed feelings about the coming week. Except Ernie. Ernie couldn't wait to get to the woods and set up camp. His grandfather had given him a brand-new rifle of his very own, and his dad was going to teach him how to shoot it.

• Chapter Two

Blam! Blam! Pow!

Bullets slammed into the trunk of the fir tree. Once in a while they even hit the homemade target George had nailed up, right at Ernie's eye level. Ernie knelt in the dirt about five yards from the tree, the rifle butt planted in his shoulder. Since Ernie couldn't keep his left eye shut, George had taped a patch of Kleenex over the left lens of his glasses. He looked for all the world like a myopic pirate, kneeling there. Every time he hit the target, never mind the bull's eye, Ernie let out a blood-curdling yelp. Every time the gun went off, his mother winced.

The tent flap opened and Sarah stuck her head out. Her eyes were puffy and her hair mussed. Nancy smiled hopefully at her daughter. 'Good morning, dear.'

'Mom, do they have to start so early? It's practically the middle of the night.'

Nancy looked at her digital wrist watch. 'Actually, dear, it's almost seven thirty.'

Sarah groaned.

Ernie ran up to the tree trunk and ripped the target down, then took it to the tent. He waved the paper in his sister's face. 'Look at that. It's practically confetti.'

'Great,' Sarah said. 'What do you move on to next – books?'

'Animals,' Ernie said. 'I'm going to get me a bear.'

'Sure,' Sarah said.

'Aw, you can't even shoot a rubber band.'

'Why would I want to?' Sarah asked. It wasn't really a question. She crawled out of the tent and squinted into the morning sun. 'Another exciting day at Camp Deerfly,' she said. 'What's for breakfast, mom?'

'The rest of us have already eaten,' Nancy told her. 'I saved you some oatmeal.'

'Can I just have some toast?'

'Of course.'

'At least I won't gain weight this vacation,' Sarah said.

Nancy handed her daughter a loaf and the toasting fork. 'The boys are going off in search of big game this afternoon. I thought maybe you and I could head off in the opposite direction and collect some wild flowers.'

'Maybe so, mom,' Sarah said. 'But I was planning to wash my hair in the creek. And if they're gone, maybe I can actually get some sleep around here.'

'We'll leave just after lunch,' Nancy said.

Sarah squatted on the ground next to the camp fire and held the toasting fork over the coals. 'Okay, as long as we're back in time for *General Hospital*.'

Nancy looked at the little portable battery-operated Sony TV set up on a milk crate next to the tent. George had given it to her for her birthday, but Nancy suspected it was really intended to keep Sarah happy in the woods. 'I wish your father had never bought that thing,' she said. 'But don't tell him.'

Ernie raced ahead. Somehow he managed to snap every twig on the forest floor. An Indian scout he wasn't. Any animal within a mile would hear him coming. Still, George smiled at his son's enthusiasm. It helped bring back his own. He remembered the summer his father had taught him how to shoot for the first time. George felt like Davy Crockett and Lewis and Clark, the great explorers, rolled into one. He bagged a squirrel. The next Christmas he'd asked for, and got, a coonskin cap. George loved that hat – so much that he insisted on wearing it in class. His fourth-grade teacher, Mrs Bundlesmith, had taken it away from him and kept it locked up in the bottom drawer of her desk until June. By then it was all squished and smelled musty. He never wore it again.

George called ahead to Ernie. 'Shhh. You have to move quietly in the woods. The idea is to surprise the animals.'

Ernie slowed down and waited for his father to catch up. 'I was being quiet.'

George ruffled Ernie's hair. Ernie squirmed. He was pretty

sure big-game hunters didn't do that sort of thing. 'Hey, dad,' he said. 'You think there're any wild boars around here?'

George smiled. 'I know there's possum,' he said.

Ernie looked disappointed. 'Aw, dad, there's possums in the city. I want to kill something really wild my first time. You know, something big.'

Ernie's blood lust made George a little bit uneasy. He decided it was time to give Ernie the talk his father had given him. 'You know, son, hunting is more than a sport. It's . . . well, it's only all right to kill animals if you eat what you kill.'

Ernie hopped impatiently in the underbrush. 'I know all that stuff, dad.'

'What I'm saying is, I don't think your mother has any recipes for wild boar.'

Ernie cocked his head back so he could look his father in the eye. 'When was the last time we had possum stew for supper?'

All in all, it was a long week. Sarah didn't hide her boredom, and she didn't get her sleep. The mosquitoes were big and swarmed around the Hendersons. Because Sarah refused to put on the Old Woodsman's Fly Dope her father had brought, she was soon covered head to toe with nasty bites. It wasn't so bad during the day, when she had the television to distract her, but she scratched all night. This kept the rest of the family, in their small tent, awake.

Ernie didn't bag his boar. On Tuesday, crouched to fire, he lost his balance when the gun went off and toppled backwards into a patch of poison ivy. George decided that, in the circumstances, it might be smarter to fish than to hunt, but the trout, full of mosquitoes, were slow to take their bait. The ones who did bite were the runts, not keepers. It was the kind of fishing that required patience. George enjoyed it – he could laze on the stream bank, his back against a tree, and sketch while he waited for a bite – but all the waiting drove Ernie crazy. Like his grandfather, he wanted results NOW. Thursday afternoon, after almost half an hour of unexpected peace, George looked downstream to see his son, waist-deep, aiming his rifle into the water.

'Ernie!' George called. 'What the hell are you doing?'

Ernie looked upstream at him. 'If you can't hook 'em, shoot 'em,' he said. Dead serious. George laughed. Ernie was offended.

When they finally did manage to catch a respectable supper, two legal trout, Sarah refused to eat them. The only kind of fish she liked came frozen and breaded from Safeway. Sarah didn't like to be reminded that her dinner had once had heads and tails. She lived the week on toast, raisins and packaged noodle mix.

Nancy was the only one of the family who enjoyed any real success. Always careful to head away from her menfolk, she roamed and climbed in search of flora. On one of her expeditions, while George and Ernie were stalking snipes and Sarah was watching the afternoon soap operas, Nancy stumbled upon a meadow bright with wild flowers. Guide book in hand, she identified cow parsley, foxglove, bleeding heart, wild iris. Carefully she pressed her specimens between sheets of wax paper and filled her pockets with them. No one else in the family thought they were the least bit wonderful. Sunday was a long time coming.

Sarah lifted the boiling kettle off the firepit and poured some into the washing-up bowl. The steam was going to make her fringe frizz. 'I don't see why Ernie never has to do the dishes,' she complained.

Nancy sighed. 'Because he does a lousy job, that's why.'

'That's no excuse.'

'Look, Sarah,' Nancy said, 'just be glad we're going home.' Nancy was profoundly glad the family vacation was drawing to a close. One more day in close quarters might cost her her sanity. She loved her children dearly, but after six nights in a four-person tent, she wasn't sure she liked them very well.

'I can't wait to get back to civilization,' Sarah said. 'By the way, do you suppose you could drive me out to Southcenter tomorrow afternoon? I've still got some school shopping to do.'

'Ask me tomorrow afternoon,' Nancy said. She crawled inside the tent, lay down and rolled across the sleeping bags to squish the air out, then stuffed them one by one, like big down sausages, into their duffle bags. She was always amazed that they fitted. Underneath the sleeping bags there was a stratum of stray socks and dirty underwear – a week's worth. These she crammed into a big plastic rubbish bag and sealed it tight against the smell. She tried to picture the laundry-room cupboard. Was there enough bleach in the whole world to get Ernie's socks white again?

Suddenly, outside the tent, there sounded a terrific scream. Sarah. Nancy crawled out of the tent, half expecting to find her daughter being hugged by a grizzly bear, only to see George and Ernie topping the rise beyond the camp site. The corpse of a rabbit dangled from Ernie's hand. When he saw Nancy, he lifted the dead rabbit aloft.

'Lunch,' George announced.

'And I killed it!' Ernie beamed with pride.

Beside Nancy, Sarah made a gagging sound. 'There's no way I'm eating a dead rabbit. You said we were leaving. Will this never end?'

The limp rabbit wiggled sadly as Ernie drew closer with his prize. Nancy put her hand on Sarah's arm. 'We are leaving. Before lunch.' She turned to George. 'What happened to "Home before dark . . . Grab a bite on the road?"'

George gave her his best 'be reasonable' smile. 'Come on, Nan, it's Ern's first kill.'

'Yeah, mom. It's my first blood.' Ernie bounced up and down in his excitement. As he did, a trickle of blood spat from the rabbit's mouth.

Nancy was pretty sure her appetite would never return. Into the look she threw George she packed all the disapproval that would fit. 'Well, I hope you're real proud of yourself,' she said.

'You're a butcher, Ernie,' Sarah said. She *sounded* disgusted, but she looked a little green around the gills.

Ernie advanced, grinning. He waved the rabbit in his sister's face. 'Back off, Sarah. It was him or me.'

Dramatically, Sarah turned her back on Ernie and his prey. 'In that case,' she said, 'I wish the rabbit had won.'

• Chapter Three

Nancy hit upon a compromise. She usually did. To make up to Sarah for one more meal *au naturel*, she promised to take her shopping the following afternoon. To George she said, 'Okay, you're right. A boy should get to eat his first kill. In fact, he should *have* to. Where's your skinning knife?'

George pulled the curved knife from the scabbard on his belt. 'Right here.'

Ernie jumped up and down. 'Oh boy. Am I hungry.'

Nancy took the knife from George and handed it to Ernie. Ernie blinked at her behind his glasses. 'Go on,' his mother said. 'You kill it, you clean it.'

'That's women's work,' Ernie said. He looked to his father. 'Isn't it, dad?'

George knew he was treading on quicksand. He could feel his wife's and daughter's eyes upon him. They were just waiting for him to say something sexist. He put his hand on Ernie's shoulder. 'Come on, son. We'll show them how it's done.'

'I'd rather not watch, thank you,' Nancy said. 'Come on, Sarah. There's some cheese left in the cooler. Let's make ourselves some sandwiches.'

Ernie liked cleaning the rabbit a whole lot less than he'd liked shooting it. He wondered if Rambo ever felt a little sick when he had to touch guts. They never showed you that in the movies. But then, Rambo killed mostly people, not rabbits. Ernie tried to think about other things while he skinned the rabbit. He thought about school starting. He thought about baseball. He thought about telling the guys about his hunting trip. In his imagination the rabbit turned into a wolf. When he looked down, it was still small, bloody and slimy in his hands. Finally, it was ready to cook.

Nancy had already doused the campfire, so George had to build a new one. There was no time to wait for coals. He skewered the rabbit and charbroiled it over open flames. For lunch George and Ernie ate charred rabbit carcass. For pride's sake, they pretended to enjoy it. When Nancy and Sarah were out of earshot, George promised Ernie they'd find a place to stop for burgers on the way home. They saved the rabbit skin so they could get it stuffed.

On the way home everyone was cranky except for Ernie, who was hyper. The station wagon was less like a passenger car than a badly packed moving van. Whenever George rounded a sharp curve, the camping gear shifted precariously. Restless, Ernie kept crawling back and forth from the back seat to the way back.

'Sit still, Ernie, and fasten your seat belt,' Nancy said. 'If a cop sees you without your seat belt, your father could get a ticket.'

'Aw, mom. That's bunk. Cops have better things to do than give kids tickets.'

In the front seat Nancy nudged George's knee. 'Your mother's right, Ernie,' George responded. 'It's the law.'

In the back seat Sarah said weakly, 'I think I'm going to throw up.'

Nancy half-turned to find her daughter looking pale. 'Open the window, honey. A little air will do you good.'

'It's the fish,' Sarah said. 'Ernie, close the cooler.'

Nancy assumed her detective voice. 'Ernie, what are you doing in the fish?'

'Looking for my baseball glove. Hey, dad?'

George looked for his son in the rearview mirror but couldn't see him around the sleeping bags. 'Yeah?'

'You think I can get a pair of real Major league type cleats when we get back?'

George grinned. One thing you had to say for Ernie – he was enthusiastic. 'You bet.'

'Great! I'm gonna spike Frankie MacDowell.'

Nancy was unmoved by Ernie's enthusiasm. 'Don't you

dare,' she said. Once again her hand nudged George's thigh. Once again George performed on cue. 'Listen to your mom, Ernie,' he said.

Ernie's voice rang with protest. 'But he spiked me twice.'

'Well, that's different. Go ahead, then.'

'George!' Nancy's voice was indignant. Her gaze burned like a laser beam on George's cheek. She was a good woman, a good mother, George thought, but there were some things she just didn't understand. In the city the differences between the sexes didn't seem to matter so much. It took a week in the woods to really bring it out. 'That's just smart baseball, Nan,' he explained, even though he knew she'd never agree.

'All right!' Ernie chirped. 'Did anybody see my baseball?'

'Just be careful of my drawings,' George called back. 'And don't step on the trout.'

'Or my flowers,' Nancy added.

'Or the flowers,' George said. He wasn't much for dried flowers, but he was glad Nancy had found them. He smiled sideways at her. 'Roughing it wasn't so bad, was it?'

Beside him, Nancy shrugged. 'You know me. Nature is growing a potato in a glass. I'm just not cut out for camping.'

George's smile deepened. Nancy always said that. Either she hated camping less than she let on, or she loved him more than she admitted. Either way, she was a brick. Much as he regretted not going to art school, George never regretted marrying Nan. At thirty-five she was still trim, blonde as ever, still fun. Even the old man had to admit she was a keeper.

The sun was low through the trees, their shadows long across the road. It was the time of day photographers call magic hour. George mellowed with the light. He was glad they'd made a late start, not just because it gave Ernie a last chance at hunting. This way they'd have the pleasure of late afternoon in the forest and hit the city after dark, when it looked its best. Seattle was beautiful on a clear night. Life was beautiful, at least until tomorrow morning. George pushed thoughts of tomorrow from his mind and studied the light. He'd have to try capturing that – the way the low sun raked through the branches of the firs.

Suddenly, a doe broke from cover and dashed across the

road. George hit the brakes. The rear end fishtailed a little, but the deer made it safely to the other side of the road. Her tail bobbed white among the underbrush before she disappeared into the trees. George congratulated himself on his quick reactions.

Nancy was tense beside him. 'George, please. Slow down.'

'Come on, Nan. I know these roads like the back of my hand.'

Nancy clutched the dashboard and peered out through the windscreen, alert as the co-pilot in a fighter plane. 'And I know Seattle will still be there if we get home fifteen minutes later,' she said.

George sighed. His peaceful mood was gone. He pressed the accelerator, just a little, and watched his wife's knuckles turn white.

'George, please.'

He glanced at the speedometer. 'I'm only doing fifty.'

'The curve-caution sign said twenty-five.'

The sign was right. Going round, the tyres squealed a little. In the back of the wagon the camping gear shifted and scattered. Coming out of the curve, they were headed due west. The sun was big and blindingly bright in front of them. Nancy slammed her visor down and rummaged through the glove box.

'George, do you need your sunglasses?'

'I'm fine, dear.'

Nancy whacked the glove compartment shut and turned her attention to the back of the wagon, via the rearview mirror. The rifle had landed squarely in Ernie's lap. Nan put on her sternest voice. 'Ernie, don't even touch that gun.'

'Rifle, dear,' George said.

'If you can shoot with it, then it's a GUN.'

In the mirror George saw Ernie grin. 'Hey, dad. Maybe there's still a chance you could blast something.'

'Ernie, don't give your dad any ideas. I couldn't face another stuffed bunny.'

'Did I bring my rifle?' George protested. 'Did I? No.' Darn sun *was* bright. He put his visor down. He put his arm around Nancy and felt her relax inside it. Her voice was softer when she said, 'You're right, George. We'll always remember this as the first camping trip that Ernie killed something and you didn't.'

George saw her head jerk up. His own eyes followed, slamming into the sun, so bright it hurt.

'Oh, my God,' Nancy said.

Something huge and dark flickered in the glare. Instinctively, George braked. Again the shape appeared, huge, black, gone. A man? It looked something like a man, but it was big. Too big. George's insides lurched. He swerved away from where he imagined the thing had gone. Then, *whap*. Even as he felt impact and heard the bumper crumple, George saw it, big and dark and manlike, rising up, hurtling away.

It, whatever it was, landed in a big black heap beside the road.

• Chapter Four

Ernie waited for somebody to say something. For a long time no one did. His dad just sat there, still as a statue, holding on to the wheel. Finally he let go and gave his head a little shake. Ernie saw him peek into the side mirror. Then his dad rolled down his window and looked out. Ernie looked too. A big furry mountain of a thing lay beside the road. It didn't move.

His dad blew out a long breath. 'My God, I thought I'd hit a man.' Ernie could tell he was glad the thing in the road wasn't human. 'Everybody all right?' his dad asked. 'Nancy?'

His mom said, 'I'm okay. Kids?' She looked around at them. Sarah was huddled against the car door, wrapped up tight in her own arms. Girls had no sense of adventure. Once Ernie realized he was in one piece, he let out a yelp of excitement. 'My first car crash. All right! Too bad you weren't going faster, dad. We could have rolled it!'

His mom was still looking at Sarah, and Sarah was still looking scared. It was obvious to Ernie that she was faking, but his mom asked her again if she was okay. Finally, Sarah nodded.

'What was it, George?' his mom asked, and his dad answered in that same funny flat voice. 'I don't know. It all happened so fast. Must be a bear.'

Ernie knew it was no bear. It was too big to be a bear. Besides, he was sure the thing had been running on two legs, not four. Bears only did that in circuses, not in the woods. His mom didn't buy the bear stuff either. 'Could it have been a gorilla?' she asked.

His dad shook his head. 'I don't think they get that big around here,' he said.

Sarah finally came back to life. She leaned forward and said,

'I think we should get out of here, daddy.' Typical Sarah, chicken through and through.

Then Ernie had an inspiration. Hitting something with a car wasn't quite the same as blasting it, but what the heck? A trophy was a trophy, right? The thing in the road was even bigger than the humongous stuffed grizzly his grandfather kept in the store, the one everybody called Claws. 'Hey,' he said, 'if Grandpa doesn't want the head, can I have it? I can keep my cassettes in it.' His grandfather had a table that was really an elephant's foot and a hat rack made out of moose antlers. For a minute Ernie pictured the thing's head in his bedroom, with tapes between its teeth.

His mom turned around and tried to see out of the back window over the camping stuff, which was impossible. 'What if it's still alive? What if it's in pain, George?'

'If it's still alive, it's probably not in a very good mood,' his dad said.

Ernie couldn't believe it. They'd just had a car crash and bagged a monster, and his folks were sitting there talking like they were trying to decide what kind of pizza to order. Grown-ups. He couldn't take it any more. 'No way it's alive,' he told them. 'You trashed him, dad. There's probably guts and eyeballs hanging off the bumper.'

Beside Ernie, Sarah shuddered. She rolled her window down fast and stuck her head outside.

What a wimp, Ernie thought. Worse yet, his dad got mad at *him*. It wasn't fair.

George's heartbeat was almost back to normal. After the rush came the shakes. His hands were slippery with sweat. Nan kept telling him they couldn't just leave it there in the road, as though 'it' was the neighbour's dachshund or something. Just pop it in the back seat and take it to the vet. No way. George had seen it with his own eyes. He had felt the front end crumple like a piece of Kleenex when they hit the thing. Whatever 'it' was, and George's best guess was a lost steer, about three thousand pounds of raw hamburg on the hoof. They weren't talking small.

'George, it could be suffering,' Nan said.

'Yeah,' George said. He sat tight. No use in doing anything hasty. There was still a possibility he might wake up. This felt too much like a dream to be real. He breathed deep, as he did when he was trying to outfox a nightmare, and tried to imagine himself back in bed. Nothing changed. Ernie was still breathing down his neck, Sarah was still gagging out of the window, and Nancy was still urging him to try first aid on a three-ton fur ball. Slowly George started the car and turned it around in the narrow road.

The thing lay smack in the middle of the road. It sort of reminded George of the guest bedroom where all the wives piled up their fur coats at Christmas parties. He kept his eyes glued to it, looking for signs of life, but it didn't move. He stopped the car and opened his door an inch or two. 'I want everybody else to stay inside.'

Wide-eyed, Nan looked at him. 'Be careful, dear.' George promised he would.

He climbed out of the car and slammed the door shut behind him. First things first. He checked out the front end and felt his heart drop into his Nikes. He'd had this car for fifteen years – just five more and they were talking genuine antique. Fifteen years and hardly a scratch on her. Fifteen years of regular wash jobs, fifteen years of Turtle Wax, and now the hood was corrugated like one of those old-fashioned washboards. All because some darn dumb animal had decided to jaywalk. For a moment George was indignant. Then he wised up. The darn dumb animal was out there with him, and it was bigger than a horse. He glanced through the windows at his family. They stared at him expectantly. You figure it out, dad. George edged towards the creature.

Were his insurance premiums paid up? Would Nancy remember where to find their will? Poor thing, she hadn't worked in fifteen years, not since Sarah was born. Actually, George didn't think dying would be so bad, but he was allergic to pain. What if the creature didn't finish him off? The heap of fur in the road didn't move, but the closer George got, the more it smelled. Sort of like the monkey house at the zoo.

Nan stuck her head out the window. 'Shouldn't we call a ranger?'

'Not yet.' Closer, closer. George kept his eyes glued to the heap. Maybe it wasn't dead, just playing possum. No sense in taking unnecessary risks. George kept his eyes on the thing as he moved around to the back of the wagon and felt inside. His own rifle, the big one, the one Nan thought he didn't bring, was carefully concealed under the family's foul-weather gear. He pulled it out and checked the chamber.

'You did bring it!' Ernie was exultant. And loud. 'Doncha need some back-up, dad?'

'No! I want you all to stay in the car.' George glanced at Nan. Her look could have fried an egg. He motioned to the creature. 'This is exactly why I brought it. Protection.'

'You didn't need to lie,' Nan said.

This was no time to argue. George didn't answer. Instead, he moved towards the creature. Again, the smell hit him. If George had had another hand, he would have held his nose. At last he stood beside the thing.

No telling which end was up. With the rifle he poked the fur ball. Nothing. Then he spotted something like an arm and, at its end, what appeared to be a paw. Paw, wrist. Wrist, pulse.

'Shoot it, dad.' Ernie's shrill boy voice broke so deep a silence it startled George. At first, he thought it might have been the creature. 'It's already dead,' he yelled back to his son.

'Shoot it anyway!'

He was going to have to have a little talk with Ernie if he made it back alive. The boy had to understand you don't just go around blasting things, Rambo and Dirty Harry notwithstanding. George crouched low enough to reach the creature's paw. The back of it was hairy, but when George turned it over, five huge fingers uncurled to show a palm that might have been his own. Well, bigger, but human. A real hand. Gently, George laid the hand back in the dirt and called his wife.

Nancy leaned out the car window. 'What is it?'

'I think you'd better come take a look.'

Ernie took that for permission too. The whole family piled out of the car. The creature's smell hit Sarah's queasy stomach, but Ernie marched right up. 'Holy Toledo,' he said. Then he apologized.

In the circumstances, George overlooked the slip. 'It's okay, Ern. I was looking for the right words myself.'

They stared at the creature. Again, Ernie spoke George's thoughts. 'Dad, do bears have fingers?'

'Maybe,' George said. 'But not thumbs.' Thumbs were important. George remembered that from biology, way back at Franklin High. Thumbs were an evolutionary signpost. Only primates and people had them.

'Dad, what if it's . . .' Ernie's voice was tight with excitement. 'You know. What if it's *him*?'

'Him?' George said. 'Him who?'

'Bigfoot,' Ernie said. 'What if it's Bigfoot?'

WHAT IF IT'S BIGFOOT? Ernie's words repeated loudly and slowly inside his father's head. George looked at the creature, at its strangely human hand. Four fingers and one opposable thumb. Well, it wasn't Mickey Mouse. 'Bigfoot,' George said aloud, considering.

That was enough for Ernie. 'Bigfoot!' he confirmed. 'Nice goin', dad. You didn't even wreck the hide or anything!'

Nancy and Sarah joined them near the corpse. 'It smells gross,' Sarah said.

As Nancy studied the creature, George could tell that she too saw its human elements. 'What is it, George?'

Good question, Nan. George had hoped she wouldn't ask, because the only answer he could think of sounded just plain looney. 'A Bigfoot, I guess,' he said. He waited for her to laugh. He sort of hoped she would. When she didn't, he said it again, inside his own head. Bigfoot. Nobody had ever seen one. God knows, they'd looked hard enough. Why, every few years some crackpot claimed to have spotted one, and whole troops took to the woods. They beat the bushes, they followed the footprints, they . . . It always turned out to be a hoax. That, or the person who saw Bigfoot turned out to be recently released from a mental hospital.

On the other hand, the legend lived on. Where had it come from? Indians, most likely. The thing in the road was certainly real – the whole family saw it – and it certainly wasn't like any other animal George had ever seen or heard of. Bigfoot? 'I don't know what else it could be,' George said. 'This is a big deal. It's a major discovery. I bet we could sell it to a museum for a lot of money, or do something like that.'

George looked at Nan. She looked as stunned as he felt and somewhat disapproving. Were those tears in her eyes? For a moment George felt guilty. But he hadn't meant to hurt the thing. It was all an accident, anybody could see that. The creature had no business running out in the road like that. Didn't Bigfoots (Bigfeet?) teach their children not to play in traffic? It wasn't his fault the thing didn't stop, look and listen before it crossed the road. And if there was profit to be had from its misfortune, well, so be it. George hoped it would be enough to pay for fixing the car.

George turned to his son. 'Ernie, you and Sarah take the stuff off the top of the car and put it in the back.' Ernie raced off. 'And tell your sister she'll have to help us lift this thing.'

Ernie was on it. 'Right, dad. I can't wait to see her face when she hears that!' Jogging back to the car, Ernie called out in his sweetest voice, 'Ohhh, Saaaahhraah . . .'

George had to smile.

Ernie figured his dad was probably the smartest guy in the whole world. Most people's dads would have just left the Bigfoot lying there in the road or called a tow truck or something, but not his father. His father walked around the thing a few times and stroked his chin and figured it all out. Now, George and Ernie, strong as they were, couldn't have lifted that Bigfoot up on to the roof of the car no matter how hard they tried, and they couldn't expect much help from Nancy or Sarah. Sarah couldn't even lift a bowling ball, much less a Bigfoot. But what they lacked in brawn his dad made up in brains. He built a pulley out of a rope and a branch and let the car engine do the work. All they had to do was guide the body up on to the roof.

Ernie stood on one side and Sarah on the other while his dad drove slowly forward. The invention worked like a charm. Up the creature came. Ernie sank his hands into the creature's fur and helped. Sarah looked like she was going to puke. The creature's head moved up, then its big arms and giant chest, then its thighs like Conan the Barbarian's. Then its feet. They were the biggest feet Ernie had ever seen. 'What do you say, dad? They must be size twenty!'

The thing must have weighed at least a ton. The bonnet buckled under it, and the rope stretched out and almost broke, but at last the thing was balanced on the roof. His dad tied it down tight, head on the hood and feet in the back, and covered the whole thing up with the tarpaulin.

'Good job, dad!' Ernie said.

His father studied their handiwork, then put his hand on Ernie's shoulder. 'Thanks, son. You know what they always say – there's more than one way to skin a cat.'

'Right, dad,' Ernie said. 'Can I help you skin him when we get home?'

His dad squeezed Ernie's shoulder, then let go. 'We'll see, son,' he said. Then he turned to Mom and Sarah. 'Well, I guess we better hit the road. All the extra weight up there is going to slow us down.'

The family settled back in the car and his dad drove off. Sarah was disgusted. Mom didn't seem exactly thrilled with the whole idea of taking a dead Bigfoot home, but Ernie was delighted. He always liked it when his dad gave him reason to be proud.

• Chapter Five

LaFleur chuckled deep in his throat. The sound that came out was something like the caw of a crow or the croak of a frog. His name may have meant 'flower', but there was nothing pretty or soft about old Jacques. Most people thought he was mad. This proved he wasn't.

'This' was a footprint, a big, clear, deep, authentic print. Six feet away, there was another. And another. The beast was running.

Ha! Let him run. He wasn't getting away from Jacques LaFleur. Not this time. This was it. Jacques patted his rifle, clean and well-oiled, as always. Loaded. He had no interest in taking the animal alive. A corpse would just as easily prove him right.

The tracks went on and on. Not even the cleverest joker could have faked such prints. For one thing, they were too far apart. And too deep – there was real weight behind them. LaFleur's heart hammered in his chest. He was running now, running towards his moment of glory. He had been waiting for it most of his life.

The tracks headed down towards the road. LaFleur had never known his quarry to head for civilization, but he wasn't about to argue with the evidence of the prints. He followed, a surefooted tracker after so many years spent in the woods. The prints led him out of the woods and on to the road. And there they stopped. Stopped dead. LaFleur looked up and down the road. He scanned the ground, but there was no trace of his prey.

Weary, LaFleur sank to his knees. Outsmarted again. Under his breath he muttered curses in his native French. And then. Then his eye settled on something interesting. Something promising. On hands and knees Jacques crawled to the spot and rubbed his hand across the surface of the road. Blood. And hair. And something else too. A skid mark on the road.

LaFleur smiled grimly to himself. Bigfoot would be his yet.

• Chapter Six

Dusk was dim and grainy. For once the kids were quiet. Nancy tried hard to think about safe, ordinary things like school lunches and bridge parties and the Japanese flower-arranging class she planned to take, but it was impossible. Her thoughts kept coming back to the thing strapped to the top of the car.

The problem was, of course, that Nancy guessed it was not a thing at all. It looked so human, it might have been a distant relative. It even had toenails. Maybe it had Bigfoot parents out there somewhere, or even Bigfoot babies. Maybe it loved them, the way she loved her kids, no matter how irritating they could be sometimes. Nancy leaned forward and stretched up a little, so she could glimpse her children in the rearview mirror. Half asleep, both of them. They both looked pale and dazed. She felt a little dazed herself.

Then an even worse thought struck her. 'Oh, George, what if it was the last one? I feel so guilty.'

'It's not like I tried to hit it, Nan. It was just luck.'

When George turned to look at her, he was smiling. His smile exasperated her. She wished she could make him understand her concern. 'What if we've just rendered an entire species extinct?' she asked him.

Neatly George sidestepped guilt. His smile became a grin. 'One of a kind. Hmmmm. This thing might be worth something.' Nancy shot him a look she usually reserved for the kids, to let them know their behaviour was out of line. George shrugged his innocence. 'Come on, Nan. It's all in how you look at it.'

Well, he had that right. She just wished George wouldn't insist on looking at it inside out and backwards.

'Well, the way I see it –' Nancy began, but she never finished telling him, because all of a sudden a big face pressed itself against the windscreen, a hairy face with two big upside-down eyes, an upside-down nose and, when it opened its mouth to growl at them, an enormous set of upside-down teeth.

In chorus, the whole family screamed. George braked. The car rocked sharply and the creature rolled off the top. When the car skidded to a stop on the shoulder, they watched the creature roll down the road away from them. Once it stopped rolling, it didn't move again.

Nancy spoke first. 'Oh, my God. It's alive.'

'Did you see those big, honkin' teeth, dad?' Ernie chirped.

Sarah said nothing. George asked Ernie to get his rifle ready.

'George, you're not going out there,' Nancy said.

George flashed her a tiny, reluctant smile. 'We can't just leave it in the road. What if it's suffering?'

Somehow, this time, Nancy was a little suspicious of George's concern.

George wasn't sure if he hoped the creature was alive or dead. A living Bigfoot was probably more valuable than a dead one – he really hadn't had time to think it through – and even though George had done his share of hunting, the idea of exterminating a rare animal didn't really appeal to him. On the other hand, if the thing *was* alive, he'd probably have to kill it before it got him. 'Ernie, pass my rifle,' he said. The stock slid over the seat back. Armed, George felt better. He got out of the car.

The thing lay motionless. George poked his rifle into its ribs, not hard enough to hurt it but enough to tickle it out of imitation sleep. When the creature didn't respond, George knelt beside it. Its big furry hand was cooling fast when he lifted it into his lap to feel for a pulse. His fingers combed through the creature's fur in search of a vein. Nothing. Just to be doubly sure, George felt along the tendons of its neck. Even for a layman, the carotid artery should be easy to find. Big animal, big pulse. No pulse. George guessed he was relieved. He called back to the family, waiting in the car. 'Dead!'

'Are you sure?' Nancy asked him through her half-closed window.

'Yes!'

'But are you really sure? Remember, you were sure before.'

George wished she'd just take his word for it. 'Nancy, I'm not a doctor. But it doesn't have a pulse, it isn't breathing, and it's as cold as a popsicle. Believe me, honey, it's dead.'

That seemed to satisfy her. Ernie rolled down his window. 'Dad, if it's dead, can I get out of the car now?'

'Sure, son,' George said. 'Everybody out. We've got to get this baby loaded.'

'Oh, George, do you think that's wise?' Nan asked him.

'Don't we have enough stuffed animals at home?' Sarah wanted to know.

Only Ernie shared George's enthusiasm for the task. Mostly without help from the ladies, they rebuilt their makeshift hoist and hefted the beast back on top of the station wagon. George tied it down with every inch of rope and chain he could find among their gear. This time he wanted to be sure Bigfoot stayed where it belonged. When he was done, he stood back to survey the job.

Ernie stood beside him and slapped George on the back, as high up as he could reach. 'Good job, dad. If it tries to go anywhere now, it's gonna have to take the car with it.'

George looked at his crippled bumper, his crumpled bonnet. Just three hours before the car had been impeccable. George looked down at Ernie. 'Oh, joy,' he said.

Ernie dreamed of baseball. His team was the same as usual, but they took the field against nine large, hairy monsters. The monsters looked more or less like people except bigger. They played without shoes and their yellow jerseys all said 'FEET'. The FEET were up to bat in the bottom of the fifth. Ernie was on the mound. He sent a fastball whizzing over the plate. The monster swung. Ernie heard bat and ball connect. The ball went sailing out of the park, probably out of the state. The bat was split in two. The monster looked at it curiously for a while before he lumbered off for first.

Ernie woke up confused. At first he thought he really might be dead, but then he recognized the towers of old newspapers and stacks of dusty tools and camping gear that lined his own garage back home. Home. Ernie leaned back against the seat and took a deep breath, trying to sort out what was real and what was dream from the strange images inside his head. Pretty soon his dad came out of the house and started rummaging around in the back for another load of stuff.

He glanced at the back seat, where Ernie was still resting his head against the window. 'Are you awake, son?'

'Yeah, dad. I think so. I was having one weird dream.'

His dad reached over the seat for another load of gear, then laid it down again. 'It's been a long day. You look beat. You want a ride to bed?'

Ernie thought about it for a minute and decided it would be all right. It wasn't like anybody was going to see them in the middle of the night. 'Sure,' he said.

His dad bent down and scooped up Ernie in his arms. Ernie wrapped his own arms around his father's neck. When his dad lifted him out of the car and stood up, Ernie saw a huge shape under the tarpaulin, lashed to the roof of the car. He whistled. 'It really happened, huh, dad?'

His dad looked at the giant lump and nodded. 'Yes, Ern. It really did,' he said.

'Wow,' Ernie said. His father carried him upstairs to bed.

• Chapter Seven

Jacques LaFleur was not used to stalking his prey by car. That was fine for those slick TV detectives, but he preferred to do his hunting on foot. Still, all the evidence suggested that his quarry was not on foot. There was nothing to do but take his car.

It was not long before the light was gone. By his best estimation, the vehicle LaFleur was following was heading west, towards the interstate highway. He too headed west, his headlights on high beam. When faster-moving traffic jammed up behind him, he swerved on to the shoulder and travelled in the emergency lane. His eyes scanned constantly, alert to any clue.

Thirty slow miles later a long set of skid marks caught his eye. He stopped the powerwagon and climbed out to investigate. Something big and rather violent had happened here, and LaFleur's instinct told him it had something to do with him. Some thirty feet west of the skid marks there was a large depression in the hard-packed roadside dirt, as if something very large and very heavy had landed there. His imagination failed him when he tried to deduce just what had occurred and how.

Darn. So close, and yet ... The site told him nothing. Nothing. Who were these people? Who? How? Why? LaFleur drew a flask from an inside pocket of his hunting vest and took a long swig, hoping the whisky would help clear his thoughts. Then he chuckled. 'Perhaps, Jacques, you expect they would leave a business card, to make your searching easy?'

Once more he aimed his flashlight down the skid mark and into the roadside brush beyond. This time he was rewarded by the glint of metal. He retrieved the object. Yes, there was blood, just as before, and hairs, a few coarse black hairs. LaFleur threw back his head and laughed a hearty laugh, deep and genuine.

The thing in his hands was almost as good as a business card, after all. It was a number plate.

• Chapter Eight

George was exhausted. Almost as soon as his head hit the pillow, he was out. But it isn't easy to sleep soundly with blood on your bumper and a Bigfoot in your garage. All night he tossed and turned, holding nightmares at bay. When his eyes popped open at 5.49 a.m., George knew he was awake for the day.

Beside him, deeply asleep, Nancy snored softly. George wished she would wake up so they could talk. He was even tempted to rouse her but then thought better of it. He didn't imagine she'd be thrilled. She hadn't wanted to bring the Bigfoot home in the first place. He was pretty sure she wasn't going to want to sell it.

On the other hand, if fate, or kismet, or whatever you wanted to call it, was going to drop a golden goose in their laps, it would be foolish not to make a profit out of the eggs. How else was George Henderson going to get rich? Not working for his father, that was sure. The old man was tighter than a ukelele string. Probably thought he could take it with him to the big-game reserve in the sky. And George was sick, just plain sick, of selling sporting goods. The more he thought about it, the more he began to believe there was a reason the Bigfoot had chosen to kamikaze against his car and not someone else's.

There had to be folks out there who'd pay a bundle for a Bigfoot hide. Look at all the people who came into the store wanting to buy Claws. And they had more to sell than just a carcass. There was their story too. Movie rights. George wondered who would play him. Paul Newman, maybe. He imagined a fat stocks and shares portfolio. He imagined Sarah's coming-out party, Ernie's graduation from Harvard.

Of course, George had no idea if his son was smart enough for Harvard – it was really too soon to tell – but it was nice to think that if he got in, they'd be able to pay his way. Nancy shifted from her back to her side and muttered something in her sleep. George wondered, suddenly, if he were being sexist. What the heck. Let Sarah go to Harvard, too. But only if she wanted to. George promised himself he would never tell *his* kids what to do with their lives. They could join the circus as far as he was concerned.

A terrible thought struck him. What if they *wanted* to be engineers or accountants when they grew up? George sighed. Much as he would be disappointed, he wouldn't interfere, even with that.

Best of all, George imagined himself in his own studio, painting all day long. If he could paint all the time, he'd get better and better until he was really good. Then he would get famous. Maybe he'd open a gallery of his own too. No sense in paying some greedy agent a fifty or sixty per cent commission to sell his pictures. Nancy could manage the gallery while he painted. If she wanted, it could be a flower shop too.

No, scratch that. He couldn't very well paint nature if he was stuck in the city all the time. Let somebody else take care of business. They'd build themselves a little A-frame house in the woods.

All that daydreaming made George impatient. He wanted it to be nine o'clock so he could start making the phone calls that would make them rich. Who should he call first? Well, time enough for that later.

It was only six fifteen. George decided to have a look at his golden goose. Not that anything was wrong – what could be wrong? Just to make sure.

He crawled out of bed and crept down the stairs, then pawed through the junk drawer in the kitchen. The torch had to be in there. Candles, keys, a hammer, a cheese grater, a roll of tape . . . Gotcha! His hand closed on the torch. Just beyond it he felt the cool casing of his metal measuring tape. Might as well get the big guy's stats straight while he was at it. He took the tape.

It was still dark outside, and just a little spooky. Those new haloid street lights made everything look green or purple. Every dog in the neighbourhood seemed to be awake and howling. Already there was a nip of autumn in the air, and George shivered in his bathrobe. When he got to the garage, he turned on the torch and shined it through the window.

The ropes were broken. The tarpaulin was thrown aside. Except for the car, which looked like it might not ever go anywhere again, the garage was empty.

Then came the crash. It was hard to imagine just what could crash so loudly. The sound came from the house. George turned towards it. A small, pale, ghostly light blinked on and off inside the kitchen. By the time George got there, the light had stopped. He dropped his torch. The dark was deep and ominous. After his eyes adjusted, he saw the shadow, huge and moving, more ominous still. More from curiosity than courage, he followed it, past the sink, past the dishwasher, past the cupboards and the ironing-board cupboard.

George found himself staring into a very large pair of very widely spaced eyes, kind of greenish-turquoise eyes, with light-brown centres. They were embedded in a very large and hairy face. It was the Bigfoot, and it wasn't dead. Apparently, it was hungry because the refrigerator lay on its side, wide open, and the Bigfoot was wearing the biggest milk moustache George had ever seen. When the creature opened its mouth to growl at George, he would have been impressed by its big white teeth if only he hadn't been so scared.

When the creature stood, George found himself looking up. Way up. The Bigfoot dropped the milk carton and reached for George. George backed away. He tried his voice, but it wasn't working very well. The creature came and he went, back, back, until he backed into the kitchen table. This time his voice worked just fine. He yelled for help. 'Somebody! Anybody! Hellllllllllllp!'

Ernie flew down the stairs. What he saw inside the kitchen stopped him short. There was his father, backed against the wall. There was the Bigfoot, amazingly, wonderfully, ENORMOUSLY alive! 'All right!' he hollered. 'I knew you weren't dead.'

'Not yet, Ernie,' his dad called back. 'Quick, get my rifle.'

'Not you, dad,' Ernie said. 'Him. He's still alive.'

'Ernie!'

'He looks so much bigger standing up.' It was true. The Bigfoot was even taller than the stuffed gorilla at the Museum of History and Industry. 'He's got you beat by a couple of feet. How tall are you, dad?'

His father yelled for help again. His mother came downstairs. 'Oh, my God! George, are you all right?'

'Nancy, get my rifle. Quick.'

The Bigfoot turned and took a good look at Ernie's mother. Ernie thought he almost looked glad to see her.

'What do you want your rifle for?' his mom asked his dad.

'Because I'm about to be eaten by a . . . by a . . .'

Ernie decided to help his father out. 'Bigfoot, dad. I think it's a Bigfoot for sure. What do you think, mom?'

His mom agreed with him. Then Sarah came in and got all worked up about the way the Bigfoot smelled. Actually, Ernie kind of liked how he smelled. His dad got mad at Sarah. 'Your father is about to be devoured by a wild, vicious, savage beast, your poor mother is obviously in a state of shock, and you complain about a smell. This is unbearable. Nancy! Do something!'

Ernie hadn't heard his dad yell so much at one time since last year's Super Bowl. He was really upset. Meanwhile his mom started to sort of inch her way towards the sink, real slow, and they all watched her do it. She called out to his dad, 'I think I know what to do, dear.' His dad seemed real glad because he obviously didn't know what to do. What his mom did was corner the room deodorizer and start spraying it all around the room. It was called Glade, and smelled just like the woods, only stronger. Ernie thought the Bigfoot kind of liked it.

Then Sarah let out one of her first-class Sarah shrieks. It was so loud even the Bigfoot stared at her. She moved towards the refrigerator, the creature and the mess on the kitchen floor. Maybe the Bigfoot thought she was playing some kind of game. He watched her as she squatted down and reached for something right in the middle of the mess. Sarah picked up an old flower that had been rotting in the refrigerator for months. The Bigfoot grabbed the box away from her. Ernie felt like cheering.

'Oh, mom,' Sarah wailed. 'My corsage.'

Then the Bigfoot did something really neat. He ate Sarah's stupid old corsage. Ernie wished he'd thought of it himself. It would have been worth the bellyache just to see that look on Sarah's face. The Bigfoot apparently thought the flowers tasted just fine, even without hot fudge.

'My orchid. My beautiful orchid. It's eating my fifteenth birthday corsage. The one I've saved for months!' Ernie had to admire his sister's lung power, even if she did use it to complain all the time. And the Bigfoot was impressed. He spat out the rest of her dumb orchid right then and there. It was too late, though. Sarah really let him have it.

'I was going to keep that flower for the rest of my life, but you've eaten it! I don't care how big and ugly and smelly you are, you can't go around eating other people's corsages. It was a *bad* thing you did. A bad, bad thing! Do you hear me?'

No way the Bigfoot couldn't hear. They could probably hear her downtown, the way she was carrying on. She certainly had his attention, Ernie had to hand her that. Then she started wagging her finger in its face, just like she always did to Ernie when she was really mad and trying to act like Mom.

'Even if you *are* an animal, you can't go around acting like one in this house.' Ernie thought the Bigfoot looked kind of sheepish, the way he always felt when his mother let him have it. The creature backed away from Sarah. But that wasn't enough for his sister. Oh, no. She threw back her head and let out a bloodcurdling scream. The Bigfoot looked her right in the eye and screamed back. He won. Sarah went running to her mother. His dad ordered them to evacuate the house.

Ernie thought the Bigfoot looked pretty confused. On his way out the door, he stopped to explain. 'She didn't mean it. All girls are weird, you know?' As his mother pushed him out into the yard, Ernie secretly hoped the creature would stay around long enough to give him some lessons in handling his big sister. With an ally like that, he'd never lose a fight again.

• Chapter Nine

The Hendersons filed into the back yard. The pre-dawn chill cooled Sarah down a little. Once she stopped being quite so angry, she realized her knees felt watery and weak. She'd just lambasted a Bigfoot. Well, he deserved it. That animal had worse manners than Ernie, and that was saying a lot.

'Boy, Sarah,' Ernie said, 'you really made him mad.'

Sarah told her brother to shut up. Maybe if they were really lucky, the beast would eat the little creep or something. Their mother told them both to shut up. The whole family gathered at the picture window to watch the Bigfoot remodel their house.

First it was the living-room door. Too low. The creature bumped its head when it tried to go through, so it just reached up, pushed, and raised the doorframe a foot or two. No problem.

'Bummer,' Ernie said.

His mom said, 'Shouldn't we run?' Nobody ran.

Bigfoot moved on to the living-room. The family scuttled around the side of the house to get a better view. They arrived in time to see the creature sampling leaves from various of their mother's fancy foreign plants. Even Ernie knew better than to mess with Mom's plants. The Bigfoot was munching them down like they were potato chips – betcha can't eat just one.

'George,' their mom hollered, 'those are my *Passiforia corriacea*!'

The Bigfoot especially liked *Passiforia corriacea*. He ate half the plant before he discovered the aquarium. So much for salad – on to the main course. He crouched down and eyed the goldfish. Through the glass sides of the tank they could see him lick his lips. At that point their mom broke the food chain. She knocked hard on the window. The creature stood up and gave them a dirty look. For a minute Sarah thought maybe he was going to smash through the glass and eat *them*, but then the beast dropped what was left of the *Passiforia corriacea*, pot and all, into the aquarium and wandered off.

What'd caught its eye was their dad's pride and joy – the dead deer with the fake eyes and big antlers that hung on the wall between the living-room and the dining-room. It was a ten-point buck, or something. Her dad thought it was a big deal, but Sarah thought it was gross. Whenever they ate dinner in the dining-room, she made sure to sit with her back to it. Otherwise it watched you eat with those sad plastic eyes. The Bigfoot tippy-toed up and tried to stroke it. When the deer didn't respond, he looked upset.

'Oh,' their father said.

Oh was right. The Bigfoot wanted to find out what had happened to the rest of the deer. He smashed his fist through the wall and felt around the other side. No good. The Bigfoot had obviously never seen a deer without a rump before. He stood under the archway between the two rooms and looked first on one side and then the other, as if he thought maybe the deer was tricking him by moving back and forth, and he was going to catch it in the act. After a while he either figured it out or decided he never would and gave up.

Then it was time to see what he could do to improve the first floor. Even from outside, they could hear the stairs splintering when the Bigfoot stepped on them.

Dad wasn't too pleased. He said, 'That's it,' in the same voice he used when Sarah and Ernie were arguing and he wanted them to stop. It was a voice that meant business – you had five seconds to obey or lose your pocket money for the week. He strode off towards the back of the house. By the time the rest of them got there, Dad was leaning their tallest ladder against the house. When it was steady, he cocked his rifle and started up.

'What's that for, George?' Mom said. 'Why don't we just call someone?'

Dad kept right on climbing. 'I know what I'm doing. I'm

not going to stand around while some animal destroys our home.'

Sometimes Ernie didn't know when to keep his mouth shut. This was one of them. 'Dad, it's not an animal.'

Dad was in no mood to be corrected for his choice of words. Mom hustled Sarah and Ernie back around the side of the house, where they couldn't get on his nerves. Sarah was glad. She didn't want to watch the showdown. 'If it goes into my room,' she said, 'I'll definitely have to burn my clothes.'

'I've got matches,' Ernie volunteered. Sarah started to punch him in the stomach, but Mom pulled them close and told them to be quiet, please.

By the time George got to the top of the ladder, the creature was already in the master bedroom, fondling the mink stole Nancy's mother had given her. When the stole didn't wake up and start purring, the Bigfoot got upset. He gave the stole a shake. This was as good a time as any. George raised the rifle, planted the butt in his shoulder. The high-powered telescopic sight brought the creature close enough for George to see the texture of his fur. Too bad about the window, but then, what was a little glass compared with an entire house? George leaned against the porch to brace himself. It was going to be an easy shot.

It was, until the ladder slipped a little and the barrel of his rifle tapped against the window glass. That was when the creature looked at him. Looked curious. Interested. Maybe a little afraid. Looked, in fact, all the ways George could imagine himself looking if their situations were reversed. The hairs of the telescopic sight crossed right in the middle of the creature's forehead. One shot and he'd be dead meat. George knew how to aim a rifle all right. The trouble was, he couldn't shoot it. Not at something that looked so inquisitive, so intelligent, so . . . human.

He lowered the rifle. George Henderson, humanitarian. Okay. So he couldn't shoot it. Now what? He looked down to check his footing and found his family staring up at him. George looked away from their questioning faces. He started to climb down.

'George!' Nancy said.

'I'm okay,' George said. His voice came out gruffer than he meant it to.

Nobody said anything as they watched their dad climb down. Sarah was glad he hadn't killed the Bigfoot. It wasn't that she had tender feelings about the stinky thing, but she hated the sight of blood and she didn't like to see her father playing Rambo. It was so uncouth. For once even Ernie had the good sense to keep his comments to himself.

Almost as soon as Dad stepped off the bottom rung, they heard a tremendous crash. It came from inside the house. Before they could go investigate, the Bigfoot came marching out into the yard, cradling something dark and furry in its arms.

'Oh, God,' Mom said. 'It's mother's stole.'

The creature crunched into the garden, trampling the tomato plants, and then knelt down and started to dig a hole. This was one strange animal. Sarah couldn't figure him out. 'What's it doing, mom?'

'It's burying Grandma's mink.'

'This is too intense,' Sarah said. It truly was. Something in her voice must have caught the creature's attention because right then it stopped burying the mink and looked at their mom. Sarah and Ernie did too.

Their mom looked guilty. 'Well, I didn't kill the poor little things.' She turned to the creature in the garden. 'Stop looking at me that way!' The creature didn't stop looking. Their mom kept trying to explain. 'Grandma didn't kill them. Some ranchers raised them, and then they killed them. They only did it because they knew someone would *buy* it.' Mom stopped talking and looked embarrassed.

Sarah decided right then and there she was never ever going to have a fur coat as long as she lived. Not even a fur collar. Not even earmuffs. The creature patted a mound of garden dirt smooth over the stole, so it could rest in peace.

While Bigfoot was busy administering the last rites to half a dozen ranch minks, George addressed the family. 'Quick! Everybody back in the house.'

They all ran for the kitchen door. It was a good plan. Except the creature decided to come in with them. He didn't feel like hanging about in the kitchen, though. He marched on into the other room and ripped George's ten-point buck right off the wall, no by your leave or anything. He carried it out the back door to the pet cemetery where the kitchen garden used to be and started digging.

George realized that if he didn't move fast, every stuffed animal in the house was going to end up six feet deep. He asked Nancy to keep an eye on the gravedigger and hustled to the den. Down came the elk. Down came the moose. Down came the young buck and the cougar.

'George, he's coming back,' Nancy called from the kitchen.

'Stall him! Show him the pasta maker!' George opened the closet door and unceremoniously stuffed his treasures inside. He hoped the Bigfoot was too unsophisticated to notice that the wall paint was darker where the heads used to be. He stashed the wolf. The closet was so full of dead animals he could barely shut the door.

'Company, George!' Nancy called out.

George caught up with the creature just as he was about to enter the den. He rubbed his hands together. 'Well, that wraps up the old funeral, huh?' The creature's nose wrinkled as he sniffed the air, but George held firm in the doorway, and pretty soon the thing moved on to the next room. He peered into the workroom George and Nancy shared. George did his drawing there, while she planted and transplanted her pet plants. Nancy was not about to let Bigfoot sample any more horticultural delicacies. 'Not in here,' she said firmly. 'George, he's not coming in here. This is my space.'

George turned to the creature. 'Sorry. That's her space.'

The Bigfoot was evidently not familiar with the concept of personal space. He sauntered past Nancy and helped himself to a handful of tasty leaves. George whispered to Nancy, 'Keep him in here.'

'Are you kidding? He'll eat all my plants.'

'So let him,' George said. He raised a mime telephone to his ear and pretended to dial. Nancy got the message. She joined the Bigfoot at her potting table, picked up a scrawny coleanthus, and offered the pot to her guest. 'Here. Try these. They are from the dimestore.'

The Bigfoot was no snob. He consumed the coleanthus and emitted a polite burp. In the doorway, Sarah clapped her hand to her brow. 'I'm dying. This is death.'

Behind his sister Ernie said, 'I know just the place for you. It's out back.'

While Sarah was slugging her brother, George made for the living-room phone as stealthily as he could. Nine-one-one answered promptly. 'Downtown, Sergeant Mancini.'

Before George could respond, the Bigfoot ambled into the living-room. For a moment he looked curiously at George and the telephone, then began to browse around among the magazines and knick-knacks. George cleared his throat and spoke quietly into the receiver.

'My name is George Henderson. I live at 437 Manning and I want to report . . .' George paused, looking for an accurate description. He settled on 'something'.

'What kind of something, Mr Henderson?'

'A *big* something. My family is in danger.'

'Mr Henderson, do you have someone in your house? A burglar? A prowler?'

The creature dangled his long fingers in the fishtank. George lowered his voice. 'Look, don't think I'm crazy, but it's Bigfoot, Sergeant.'

Even from downtown, he could hear Mancini's long exhalation. His voice changed from serious to seriously sarcastic. 'Well, of course, pal. They sure can be a nuisance. Tell you what, Mr Henderson. Run a hose on him, he'll melt right down.'

The creature's hairy fingers closed around a goldfish. He plucked it deftly from the tank and popped it in his mouth. George bellowed, 'Hey!'

'Ouch,' Mancini said.

'Sorry, Sergeant. Look, I hit a Bigfoot with my car. I thought it was dead. I was going to call you guys in the morning. But it must have been hungry because I found it in the kitchen.'

'Whoa. Back up a minute. You hit a Bigfoot with your car? In your kitchen?'

'No. I mean yes.' George was getting seriously confused. And if he was confused, Mancini must be in far worse shape. He tried again. 'I'm under a lot of stress here. I mean, it wasn't dead any more. It just walked into our kitchen. It was eating out of our refrigerator, then I thought it was going to eat me, but it ate my daughter's corsage instead, and then a *Passifora corr . . .*, well, one of my wife's exotic plants, and it has just eaten our goldfish.' George was glad he wasn't under oath. Nancy's look told him he was being something less than coherent. Well, let her try to tell it straight.

'And where is it now, Mr Henderson?'

George wanted to give accurate testimony. The Bigfoot was headed for the bathroom. 'In the bathroom,' George reported.

'Of course, how stupid of me,' Mancini said. Then his voice got very no-nonsense. 'Look, this has gone far enough. Let me explain something to you. The charge for creating a nuisance over the telephone isn't worth the paper work involved. So, let's say I believe you have a Bigfoot in your house. First, we cordon off your neighbourhood. Second, we evacuate your neighbours. Third, we'd send a truckload of cops to deal with the thing.'

George started to protest, but the crash from the bathroom stopped him. A few seconds later the Bigfoot emerged from the bathroom. He was carrying the medicine cabinet and making faces at himself in the mirror. Meanwhile the cop talked on.

'And I mean fully armed and ready, Mr Henderson. So, unless you want to be responsible for wrongfully turning your neighbourhood into a war zone, a charge that is *well* worth the paper work, I suggest you drop the whole thing right now.'

The Bigfoot held the medicine cabinet in his left hand. With the fingers of his right, he lifted his upper lip to get a better look at his teeth. He must have thought they looked pretty good. He seemed to be smiling.

'A war zone,' George said.

'Very well, then . . .'

'Huh? Oh, no, Sergeant. No Bigfoot here. Just a bad joke.' George felt the eyes of his family on him. The Bigfoot looked too. George had the feeling they thought he'd blown it. There was no telling what the policeman thought. George tried to undo the damage. 'Look, I'm sorry. Actually, I'm not even George Henderson. Just a prank. I'm really sorry. Thanks for being so understanding. Thank you. You must have the wrong number. Goodbye.' George talked as fast as he could and hung up even faster.

Nancy gave him one of those mocking looks he'd always hated. 'If you aren't George Henderson, just who are you? Superman?'

Actually, George felt like the Lone Ranger. And he'd always believed policemen were his friends. Another childhood myth down the tubes. If the best they could do was send out a SWAT team to blow Bigfoot away, he was better off without their help. On to Plan B. There was only one problem – George had absolutely no idea what Plan B was.

He looked into the expectant faces of his family. Even the Bigfoot looked back with absolute attention. 'We're on our own,' George told them.

• Chapter Ten

'I guess the cops aren't coming, huh, dad?' Ernie said. He was glad. The police would probably have taken the Bigfoot away, just when things were getting interesting. Now that Ernie wasn't afraid of the big guy any more, he was looking forward to getting to know him better. Maybe they could keep him. Ernie imagined the Bigfoot walking him to school every day, waiting for him when the bell rang every afternoon. He could even come to all their baseball games. Like a mascot.

His father shook his head. 'At least, I hope not.'

From the expression on his dad's face, Ernie guessed this wasn't the right time to ask him if they could keep Bigfoot for a pet. When the phone rang, they all jumped. His dad answered.

'No Bigfoot here, Sergeant. What? Oh, hello, Irene. Just fine. We had a wonderful time. You're what? No, wait . . .' His dad stared at the receiver. 'She hung up. It was Irene. She's bringing Little Bob back.'

Ernie's mother looked out the window. 'It's the crack of dawn, George.'

His father shrugged. 'I couldn't stop her.'

Ernie sympathized. Nobody could stop Mrs Moffitt. He could never stop her from tousling his hair or pinching his cheeks. She thought he was cute. Ernie thought she was too much. She was always on some weird new diet, and she always wanted to tell you all about it, whether you wanted to hear or not. Thanks to their next-door neighbour, Ernie was the only kid in fourth grade who knew exactly how many calories there were in eggplant pâté. Mrs Moffitt never lost any weight either. Ernie figured the only thing that would help would be sewing her mouth shut for a month or so.

His mom sprang into action. 'I'll go meet her halfway.'

It was too late. They could hear Mrs Moffitt knocking and Little Bob barking outside the front door.

'Just take the dog and get rid of her,' his dad said.

'Easy for you to say,' his mom said. 'This is Irene Moffitt, remember? Our live-in neighbour.'

Little Bob was barking like crazy outside the door. The Bigfoot started for the door, as if he was going to let him in, but then the doorbell rang. Bigfoot didn't know about doorbells. The ringing stopped him dead.

'Oh, my God,' Ernie's dad said. 'What are we going to do with this thing?' He looked at the Bigfoot. 'No offence.'

By this time Ernie could see Mrs Moffitt trying to peek in through the curtains on the window by the door. 'It's no use hiding, Nancy. I know you're in there.'

'I could take him up to my room,' Ernie volunteered.

His mom looked at the smashed stairs and shook her head. 'The basement,' she said.

That suited Ernie. He didn't care where they were going, as long as he got the creature to himself for a while. He reached out and took the creature's hand. It was big. Ernie tugged on it. 'The basement. You'll love it down there. It's like a cave, only with a pool table.' The Bigfoot started to follow him. Ernie turned back to his dad. 'It's okay if I teach him to play pool isn't it, dad?'

His father nodded. The doorbell rang again. Then Mrs Moffitt popped up at the side window, snooping. The woman was a terrible snoop. His mother said so.

'Just a minute, Irene,' Mom called out.

Sarah leaned against the wall as if she was going to faint or something. 'This is it,' she said. 'The beginning of the end. Mrs Moffitt will see it, the whole world will know and I'll be a social outcast for the rest of my life. I'll go to the prom and the kids will throw pig's blood on me.' She looked at their father. 'Thank you, dad.'

'Cheer up,' Ernie said. 'You'd be a social outcast anyway. At least now you have an excuse.'

'Mom,' Sarah wailed, but Mom wasn't listening. Mrs Moffitt knocked again, at the window this time.

'Come on, big guy,' Ernie said. 'We don't want her to see us.'

The Bigfoot stopped walking and looked curiously at the window. 'No, no. You don't want to see her either,' Ernie told him. 'She's a creep.' Ernie looked over his shoulder at his mother. She didn't like him bad-mouthing grown-ups, even if what he said was true, but this time she wasn't listening. She and his dad were too busy pulling the curtains shut.

Ernie led the Bigfoot into the kitchen. There was food and garbage all over the floor. As they passed the sink, the Bigfoot reached out and snared an African violet from the windowsill. He was about to munch it down when Ernie's mom caught him. 'Oh no, you don't.' She looked around the mess and picked up a head of lettuce that had been in the refrigerator since before they went on vacation. It looked pretty sad, all brown and limp. 'Here, eat this.' Mom grabbed her plant and handed the lettuce to the Bigfoot. He stared at the wilted lettuce, sniffed it, then tossed it back on the floor. Ernie chuckled. This Bigfoot was nobody's fool.

'Hurry up, Ernie,' his dad called. Ernie pulled the creature towards the basement door. When he saw the steep steps with no railing, the Bigfoot stopped cold.

'It's okay,' Ernie told him. 'Come on, big guy. Follow me.' Ernie raced down the stairs. He'd just reached the bottom when the Bigfoot arrived beside him, on his butt. The stairs rained down around them, and years of dust rose up. The Bigfoot sneezed. Ernie heard his mom calling from the top of the stairs. 'We're okay, mom,' Ernie hollered. 'It was just the stairs.'

Dust settled like dandruff on the Bigfoot's dark fur. He sneezed again, at hurricane force. Ernie felt sneeze droplets spray his face. They fogged his glasses. 'Sorry about the stairs,' he said. 'You know, if you're gonna stay around here, you might want to think about losing a little weight.'

The Bigfoot didn't look too happy with this suggestion. Ernie punched his mammoth shoulder. 'Joke,' he said.

George slammed the basement door while Nancy opened the kitchen door. Nancy winced at the sight of Irene's bathrobe. It was louder than a brass band. Her hair was still in curlers. She stood expectantly in the doorway, Little Bob in one hand and the week's mail in the other. Little Bob jumped down from Irene's arms and headed straight for the basement door.

'Little Bob must be on heat,' Irene said. 'Every dog in the neighbourhood's out there.'

Nancy stuck her head out of the door and saw it was true. There was a whole pack gathered in the backyard, little dogs, big dogs, you name it. Hard to believe that Irene had kept Little Bob for a week without noticing he was a boy. Nancy thanked God for small blessings. 'Yeah,' she said. 'I guess we better take him . . . uh, her . . . to the vet.' Nancy shut the kitchen door behind Irene and swooped down to pick up Little Bob. 'Take it easy, little guy – uh, little girl.'

Sarah and George had fallen into a defensive line to block Irene. Nancy fell in beside them. Irene strained to see past them. Her nose wrinkled. 'God! What is that smell?'

She stepped up to Nancy. Nancy moved aside, letting Irene see the kitchen in all its glory. 'What the hell has happened here?' Irene demanded.

'We were just defrosting the fridge,' Nancy said. Discreetly, she elbowed George.

'Oh, yeah,' he said. 'Spoiled food. We had a little trouble moving it out.'

George was such a champion of understatement. Still, Nancy couldn't come up with a better lie. She smiled nervously at their neighbour.

Irene surveyed the battle scene, then looked searchingly at the Hendersons. 'Is everything okay with you kids?' They didn't have to answer because Irene had already moved on to the next question. Now she was crouching down, searching through the wreckage on the floor. 'Nan, I don't suppose you've got any peanut butter and brewer's yeast? I found a new diet . . .'

Nancy handed Little Bob to George and knelt beside Irene, searching. She thought they had some peanut butter. She hoped. 'Sarah,' she said, 'how about taking Little Bob out of here?'

Sarah disappeared with the dog. After some serious digging, they managed to exhume a half-full jar of peanut butter.

Nancy picked it up and read the label. 'Crunchy. This is the best I can do. No yeast.'

Irene seized the jar and clutched it to her flowered robe. 'No matter. Got to go to the market for tabasco and cod-liver oil anyway.' She patted George's stomach. 'It's an energy diet. You might want to try it.'

Accompanied by a loud cracking sound, the floor buckled upwards under George's feet, then collapsed. George responded to Irene's inquisitive look by dipping deep into a kneebend. One, two, three. 'Exercise, Irene. That's the only diet. Plenty of energy here.' Up and down he went until the floor levelled out. Nancy went to stand beside him and flashed their neighbour her biggest smile.

Irene sniffed the air. 'Probably rotten meat or eggs.'

'Just what we thought,' George said. 'Well, no use standing here breathing it.'

'Yeah,' Nancy said. 'Sure glad we could be of help, Irene. And thanks so much for taking care of Little Bob. He just hates camping.'

'No problem,' Irene said. She and the peanut butter made for the door. George smiled hopefully at Nancy. Just then the crash came.

Bigfoot loved the basement. He studied the washing machine and drier for a while, and then sat down on one. Luckily it was the heavy-duty drier. The top hardly caved in at all. 'Not too soft, huh?' Ernie said. He took the creature's hand again. 'Come on, there's something I wanna show you.'

What Ernie had in mind was the pool table, but the creature spotted the hot-water heater first. Ernie's dad had wrapped it with insulation to save electricity. Ernie had to admit it looked like a fat lady with no head. The Bigfoot thought so too. He put his big arms around her and squeezed. Suddenly the fat lady had a waist. Then he lifted her up. Ernie saw the pipes that ran up from the top of the tank squish like cooked spaghetti against the ceiling. He wasn't sure exactly where the pipes came out upstairs, but . . . Then he noticed the pool that was forming around their feet. 'You better put it down now,' he advised.

The creature gave Ernie a look that said, 'Why?'

'It's the water heater,' Ernie explained. 'No hot water, no baths. I wouldn't mind, but my mom would probably get real mad.'

The creature dropped the heater. Ernie could hear his mom screaming. 'Ernie! Oh, my God!'

He called up to her. 'Yo! It's okay. Everything's okay.'

They'd just finished explaining to Irene that Ernie had his science project in the basement when water started to pour out of the kitchen taps. It poured full-blast, hit the dishes in the sink and shot up like a fountain. George worked the taps, trying to shut them off.

'So, when are we going to play cards?' Irene asked.

'Saturday, I suppose,' Nancy said. She tried to sound casual. It sure was hard to sound casual with a flood in the kitchen. 'Same as always,' she said.

Ernie upturned a whole laundry basket full of dirty towels on top of the place where the water was coming in, to slow down the flood. By the time he'd done that, Bigfoot had discovered the furnace. He especially liked the big round metal tubes that carried the heat around the house – so much so that he decided it would be fun to swing from them. Ernie could hardly blame him – he'd always wanted to try it himself. But the creature outweighed Ernie by a good three hundred pounds. The duct gave way as though it was made of cardboard, leaving a big hole gaping in the ceiling. Curious as ever, the Bigfoot stuck his hairy hand inside.

Ernie looked around the basement. It looked almost as bad as the kitchen. And his mother said *he* was a slob. 'Oh, brother,' he said to the creature. 'I hope they don't blame me for this.'

Nancy had almost backed Irene out the kitchen door when the door came flying off the laundry chute beside it. A low growl echoed up from the depths of the basement. From the laundry chute emerged a large, hairy hand.

Nancy flung open a cabinet door to block Irene's view, then

collected every dishtowel in grabbing distance and stuffed them, and the hand, down the chute.

'What was that all about?' Irene wanted to know.

Nancy was at a loss, but George came through. 'Ernie's project. The one we were telling you about. He's got one of those, uh, gerbils.'

'Oh, yes!' Nancy joined in. 'It's such a cute little thing. Kind of like a . . .'

George contributed 'hamster'. Nancy saw the hand emerge again. As inconspicuously as possible, she cornered the last of her African violets and put it in the Bigfoot's hand. The hand withdrew. 'But bigger than your average gerbil,' Nancy said. 'And always hungry.'

'Nothing more than rats getting a lucky shake from society, if you ask me,' Irene said. She looked appraisingly at George and Nancy, then smiled. 'I know where you are if I need you.' Grasping the peanut butter, she left at last.

Ernie figured Mrs Moffitt must have finally gone home. Just in the nick of time too, while they still had some basement left. He went to where the stairs used to be and found his father looking down at him. His mother appeared beside him. 'What was all that racket?' she wanted to know.

'Well, uh, I was trying to teach him to play pool. Only I guess he got curious about where the little balls went, you know. I think he thought they went up.'

Ernie's father lay down on the floor and reached his hands down to Ernie. 'Grab my arms, son, and I'll pull you up.'

Ernie tried to grab, but something was too short – either Ernie or his father's arms. Ernie turned to the Bigfoot. 'Hey, fella, how about a lift?' The Bigfoot's hands closed gently around Ernie's waist. Seconds later, he was flying up towards his dad. When he got level with the door frame, his mom grabbed him and pulled him into the kitchen. 'Thanks,' Ernie hollered down.

His dad was still lying on his belly when the Bigfoot chinned himself on the kitchen floor. For a minute, they were eyeball to eyeball. Ernie thought he saw the creature smile.

• Chapter Eleven

'Sooooup is good fooooood,' a syrupy voice crooned, six times louder than anybody should be allowed to sing, except in the shower. George winced. That meant it was six forty-five, the time he normally hit the kitchen to make the morning coffee. It also meant that nobody had remembered to turn the timer off before they went on vacation. The TV had been playing to an empty house all week.

'Turn that thing off,' George begged. He never could understand why they advertised things like soup in the morning, when all you wanted was a cup of coffee. It made him sick to think of soup so early.

Nancy turned off the TV and George settled back to enjoy the silence. No telling how long it would last. Not long. He remembered it was Monday. 'Oh, my God. What am I going to do about work?'

'That's easy,' Nancy said. 'You're going to call in sick.'

'Can I be sick too?' Ernie asked.

'I think you and Sarah would be safer at school.'

'Awww.' Then Ernie brightened. 'At least I can tell all the kids my dad creamed a Bigfoot.'

That was all George needed. 'You're both sick,' he said. 'We're all sick. Nobody's going anywhere until we figure out what to do.' He looked towards the basement, where the creature had retreated after his peep into the kitchen. Except for the distant sound of water dripping, all was quiet. He called it quiet. What was a little water? 'Well, at least for now, it seems to be trapped down there.'

But George was wrong. The creature picked that moment to untrap itself. Must have been lonely. It chinned itself on the threshold as easily as Ernie might have on the playground bars. Little Bob sped across the linoleum at full tilt, barking his head off at the invader. The mutt was braver than he was smart. He raced right up to the creature's giant jaws, proclaiming his territory. When the creature roared back, Little Bob went into a backwards skid that sent him smack into the dishwasher. The creature stood up and surveyed the scene.

Sarah came racing into the kitchen, apologizing for losing Little Bob. 'It's okay,' George said. 'She's gone.' He turned to find the creature looking expectantly at him. 'How are you doing?' George asked.

The creature cocked his head and looked at George. He answered the question with a low, throaty sound that seemed pleasant enough.

Just then Little Bob attacked again. He made for the creature, yipping like mad, jumping higher than George had ever seen him leap, even for treats. The creature looked annoyed. He extended his hand and plucked Little Bob right out of the air. 'George,' Nancy whispered, but George shook his head. The creature's grip was gentle as he held the squirming, yapping dog in front of him. He was equally gentle when he closed his other hand around Little Bob's muzzle. Bob was persistent, even if he was a nuisance. He kept on barking inside the creature's palm.

The creature looked directly at George. Plain as day, his look said, 'How do you stand it? Is he always like this?'

George shrugged. 'Beats me.'

Suddenly it struck him that he was communicating with the creature. They'd just exchanged two sentences, clearly as if they'd spoken. The Bigfoot *was* intelligent. George looked at the rest of his family to see if they'd noticed. They had. They were all looking at George as if he were crazy, all except for Ernie, who was grinning.

Nancy stepped towards the creature, then locked eyes with him, reached out and took Little Bob in her own hands. She stroked and murmured reassurances to the dog until he quietened down and settled peacefully into the crook of her arm. The Bigfoot watched closely. When Little Bob was quiet at last, he reached out and gently patted the dog's head. Safe with Nancy, Little Bob didn't even growl.

Nancy shifted Little Bob and reached out to take the creature's hand. 'Look, George, he's hurt himself.'

'Musta been when he tried to chin himself on the heating pipes,' Ernie said.

The Bigfoot tried to pull his hand away, but Nancy held on tight. 'Ernie, get the first-aid kit, would you?' To the Bigfoot she spoke in a lower voice. 'It's okay, fella, we'll have you fixed up in no time.' The creature surrendered himself to Nancy's care. George smiled. If he was crazy, at least he wasn't alone.

Nancy looked around for a place for Bigfoot to sit while she worked on his injured hand. The chairs were too fragile, and she didn't want to risk the counters. Finally, she settled him on the kitchen floor, with his back against the refrigerator for support. Nancy was glad to see his cuts weren't too deep. He was patient while she washed them out with soap and water.

Ernie returned with the first-aid kit. After a week's camping, it was hopelessly disorganized. The only antiseptic Nancy could find was iodine. 'Are you sure we don't have anything that doesn't sting?'

'Sarah used up all the Bactine on her mosquito bites,' Ernie said. He handed his mother the iodine. 'This is it.'

Nancy spoke soft and low to the Bigfoot, a kind of singing. She recognized the voice as one she hadn't used much since her kids got older. 'Now this might hurt, just a little.'

The creature was nearly hypnotized into trust when Ernie piped up. 'What I do is just close my eyes real tight, like this.' He demonstrated the technique.

Nancy smiled. Ernie *did* do that when he was the patient. He had since he was a toddler. She soaked a gauze pad with iodine and took the creature's hand. He looked at her sheepishly, then squeezed his eyes shut tight. 'It's okay, it's okay,' Nancy crooned. Still, she felt the creature's hand wince when the iodine stung his cuts. 'Okay, it's okay, easy, boy. It's okay.'

'Does this mean we can keep him?' Ernie asked, in a voice that was unusually quiet for Ernie.

'Grow up!' Sarah said.

George said, 'Maybe . . . I don't know.' He said it with the hint of a question mark at the end.

Nancy looked up from her doctoring. 'You don't know? The answer's no. Now you know.'

'It was just so different when he was dead,' George mused.

Nancy looked sharply at him. 'No, George. *You* were different. And I was convinced it wasn't dead.'

Sarah spoke up. 'I thought we were going to sell it and get rich.'

'Let's *keep* it and get rich,' Ernie suggested.

'I can't *believe* this family,' Nancy said. What she couldn't believe was their insensitivity. Oh sure, she was always the bleeding heart, always the soft one, but somebody had to be. Enough was enough. The Bigfoot growled, and Nancy realized she'd been playing too rough with the iodine. 'I'm sorry,' she told him. She stopped dabbing and let her family have it. 'We're talking about a living, breathing being here. It might even be some kind of person.'

'It's a Bigfoot person,' Ernie said. He seemed eager to redeem himself. Nancy smiled faintly to herself. Maybe there was hope for her son yet. Just a glimmer.

'We don't know what it is,' George said. 'We don't even know if it's male or female.'

'It's definitely male,' Sarah said.

'How could you tell?' Nancy asked. Immediately she regretted the question. 'Never mind,' she said. 'I don't want to know.'

As she rose, Nancy raised an eyebrow at George – did you catch that? His face told her he hadn't; his mind was a million miles away. Slowly, he spoke. 'Nan, I don't know how, but we've got to find a way to keep this thing. It's worth big bucks. Don't you see? This is a ticket to a better life.'

What Nancy saw was trouble for everyone involved. What *was* George thinking of? Sometimes, big as he was, he was as much a little kid as Ernie. She spoke to her husband as she might have to her son. 'A better life for whom? What about *his* life?'

Her plea for common sense was lost on George. He was still building castles in the clouds. 'I'm thinking about us,

Nan. I just need time to figure a way . . .' His voice trailed off. For a moment, he was silent, figuring. Then he looked speculatively at the creature. 'At least he's safe here,' George said, and Nancy sighed.

• Chapter Twelve

LaFleur was pleased at the screech of his tyres as he pulled into the parking lot of the Bigfoot Museum. He liked to make an entrance. The place was a dump – in even worse need of paint than the last time he'd stopped. Well, that might be changing soon. LaFleur patted the pocket of his hunting waistcoat and climbed out of the cab.

Old Doc Wrightwood pretended he hadn't heard Jacques coming. He too looked shabbier than last time, if that were possible – tired and tattered. Jacques thought he was even wearing the same clothes, an ancient flannel shirt and trousers that bagged around his thin legs. 'It's an ill wind,' Doc greeted him.

'*Bonjour* to you. You won't find the wind so ill when you see what it's brought you.' With that, Jacques pulled the baggie out of his waistcoat pocket and waved it at the old man.

'What have you got in there?' Wrightwood asked him.

'What would you say to Sasquatch hairs?' With a flourish, Jacques handed the bag to Wrightwood. 'The real thing. You shouldn't have given up, Doc.'

'We may be old, Jocko, but we still aren't friends.' Doc examined the contents of the baggie for a moment, then turned to one of the tacky bear-fur Bigfoot statues he sold as souvenirs and snatched out a few hairs. 'And the only difference between these and those is that I get a buck a strand for mine.'

LaFleur snatched back his baggie and waved it under the old man's nose. 'These are real, Doc! I chased a set of tracks that ran for two, three miles.'

Wrightwood's canny old eyes narrowed. 'Okay, Jock. If

you've got real hairs, I'll buy 'em. But let's keep the price on the ground.'

Doc wandered off among the claptrap. Jacques followed. 'For Pete's sake! I almost had him.' LaFleur shook the baggie under Doc's nose. 'These are real! I almost had him. I was that close.'

'Yeah? And then what happened? Your gun jam? Or maybe a change of heart? You had him in your sights and you couldn't do it? What's the story this time?'

'I think he was hit by a car,' Jacques said.

'Well, then. That should have made it easy.'

'I know,' Jacques mused. 'But there was no trace, no tracks. Nothing. It just vanished.'

Doc Wrightwood snorted. 'Well, Jocko, it's like I tell my customers – Bigfoot eat their dead.'

'I don't know why the hell I bother.' LaFleur spat out the words.

'Because you figure I'm the only one who, deep down, wants to believe you.' Wrightwood set his jaw and looked Jacques in the eye. 'But I don't. Not any more.'

LaFleur headed for the door. He was angry with himself for coming at all. Wrightwood always made him mad, and this time was no exception. 'You know the difference between you and me, old man?'

'Where shall I start?' Doc shot him a sour grin. 'With your famous quote – "If the only way to prove that an endangered species exists is by killing one, I would not hesitate to pull the trigger"? The difference, Jocko, is Philosophy. That's with a "P".'

Pompous old goat. Jacques seethed with aggravation. 'You can throw around all the two-dollar words you want, but the answer is simple. Guts. We've both spent our whole lives chasing after that beast, and we've both had to stare at ourselves in the mirror every morning and say, "I'm not a fool." The difference between us is – you blinked.'

'Or finally opened my eyes.'

Smug old fool. Jacques was going to enjoy showing him. He was going to enjoy it a *lot*. 'We'll find out soon enough,' he said. It was both a promise and a threat.

'Go for it, Jock,' Doc said. 'Raise a ruckus. God knows, I could use the business.' He turned away from Jacques.

The sight of his stooped shoulders inside the faded flannel shirt made Jacques even more exasperated. How many years was it now they had been baiting each other? Decades. And yet there was no respect between them, no admiration. All they shared was an obsession. It was enough to keep them bickering for thirty years. Jacques smiled grimly to himself. Soon the long argument would be over. And he was going to win.

He looked at his watch. Just time to make it to Seattle, provided he didn't get snarled up in traffic. 'I have to go now,' he said to Doc. '*Au revoir.*'

'Same to you, Jocko,' the old man said.

The traffic was good to him. No breakdowns on the freeway. No accidents. Downtown, Jacques wasted no time looking for a parking meter. This time he treated himself to a car park. It was ten minutes to five when he arrived, panting, in the Washington State License Bureau.

The clerk, in her bureaucrat's cage, was about twenty-five, with fingernails too long to be real and a look of limited intelligence. Jacques spilled out the story he'd been practising. 'I was driving along the freeway, and all of a sudden I saw an old army buddy in the fast lane. I haven't seen my friend in thirty, forty years. Not since Okinawa. I honked my horn, I waved my arms, but he didn't see me. Then the idea came to me. His number plate!'

'You got the number?'

Jacques handed her a neatly folded piece of paper. 'Here it is.'

The clerk took it, then began to type something on her computer terminal. Jacques couldn't believe it was going to be so easy. He had been afraid that only policemen and insurance companies were allowed to trace parties through their number plates. And maybe bill collectors. The clerk hadn't even listened to his elaborate lie.

Only a few seconds after the clerk punched in the numbers, the computer responded with a rapid rat-a-tat-tat. When it fell silent, the clerk ripped off the printout and handed it to Jacques. 'That'll be ten bucks,' she said.

LaFleur handed over the cash and looked down at the paper she'd given him. The car was a 1971 four-door station wagon, registered in the name of George F. Henderson. LaFleur couldn't believe his luck. Henderson lived right here in Seattle. Jacques chuckled under his breath as he left the License Bureau. '*Bonsoir*, M. Henderson,' he said. '*Comment ça va?*'

• Chapter Thirteen

George stood by the phone and tried to think sick for a few minutes before he dialled. He was calling early in the hope that his father hadn't arrived yet, but it was the old man himself who answered. George wasn't sure his dad bought his story about 'a touch of the flu – or maybe it was something we ate'.

'Well, take care of yourself,' his father said. 'Casting rods go on sale tomorrow. I need you here.'

'I'm headed back to bed right now,' George assured him. 'I'm sure this will blow over soon.'

'It better,' his dad said. He hung up.

'So how's old Rough-and-Ready?' Nancy asked.

'Let's put it this way,' George said. 'I'm glad he couldn't see my face. I never could put anything over on him, you know. That guy can make me feel like I'm still ten years old.'

Nancy smiled sympathetically. 'So, are you feeling better, dear?'

George looked around the kitchen and sighed. 'Nothing a couple thousand bucks' worth of carpentry wouldn't cure.'

'Cheer up,' Nancy said. 'You've got all day to work on it.'

'Actually,' George told her, 'I really was thinking about going back to bed. You know how I hate to lie.'

Nancy let fly with the dishrag she'd been using to mop out the refrigerator. 'Don't even consider it,' she said. 'Not when there's no hot water.'

'No what?'

'Read my lips,' Nancy said. She spoke slowly and loudly, as she would to a small child or a dumb animal. 'NO HOT WATER.'

George groaned. Nancy continued in her dog-trainer mode. 'WE NEED HOT WATER.'

'I'll have a look downstairs,' George told her, 'as soon as I figure out how to *get* downstairs. By the way, where's our house guest?'

'With Ernie,' Nancy said. She consulted the kitchen clock. 'I think they're watching *Sesame Street*. Ernie thought Bigfoot might get a kick out of seeing Big Bird.'

George wished he'd worn his waders into the basement. Already his Nikes were wet and squishy inside. The hot-water heater had been totally uprooted. It was pinched in at the middle and lying on its side. In the basement gloom, it closely resembled a headless corpse. 'Sorry about that, old girl,' George mumbled. 'No showers for a while.'

Cautiously, he moved the mound of soggy bath towels and uncovered the source of the underground spring. George was a pretty good handyman – he'd installed the double-glazing by himself and built Nancy's greenhouse – but this job was beyond him. It called for a professional. The best he could do was shut the water off until the plumber came. As he battled the rusty valves with his wrench, George tried to remember what their insurance policy said about natural disasters.

When he'd done what he could to restore order in the basement, George set up his painter's ladder and climbed into the kitchen. 'I've got good news and bad news,' he told Nancy.

'Tell me the good news first,' she said.

'Okay. We've still got a basement.'

'And the bad news?'

'We've also got a pool.'

Sarah stormed into the kitchen. She was still wearing her bathrobe, and her hair looked like a caesar salad, tossed and oiled. 'Daddy,' she wailed. 'What's wrong with the shower? When I tried to turn the water on, nothing happened.'

'That's a relief,' George said. 'I guess I found the shut-off valve.'

'The shut-off valve! Daddy, I just put Damage Pak Twenty-Minute Conditioning Treatment on my hair. What am I going to do?'

'Have very well-conditioned hair, I guess,' George said.

Sarah turned to her mother. Nancy turned to George. 'You could have warned us first,' she said.

George counted to ten, then twenty, before he spoke. 'I'm sorry,' he said.

'You should be,' Sarah said. 'How am I ever going to get this gunk out of my hair?'

'You could turn on the sprinklers,' George suggested. 'I think we've still got water outside.'

Sarah glowered at her father and marched out of the back door.

George had just finished patching the wall between the living-room and the dining-room when Nancy called the family to lunch. Bigfoot followed Ernie into the kitchen, sniffing the air. When Ernie and George pulled out their chairs, the Bigfoot mimicked them. He was about to sit down when Nancy caught him. 'No,' she shrieked, then lowered her voice. 'I mean, you sit over there.' She pointed to a spot on the floor.

The Bigfoot looked offended. Ernie patted his arm. 'I'll sit by you,' he said. 'That's okay, isn't it, mom?'

'As long as it keeps him happy.' Nancy sighed. Ernie and Bigfoot sat on the floor. Nancy put steaming bowls before them. 'Alphabet soup,' she said. 'Don't worry. It's vegetarian.'

Nancy had put the creature's lunch in a serving bowl, but it still looked absurdly dainty in his hands. He lifted the bowl to drink, but the rising steam tickled his nose. 'It fogs up *my* glasses,' Ernie told him. 'You've got to wait for it to cool down.'

Sarah came late to lunch, a towel wrapped around her head. 'Mom, does he have to eat in the kitchen?'

'I thought about taking him to McDonald's,' Nancy said, 'but I was afraid he'd try to climb the golden arches.'

'That's not funny, mom,' Sarah said.

'Thanks, Sarah,' Nancy said.

'First, you slurp it in like this,' Ernie instructed. 'Then, when all the soup's gone, you can play with the letters.' Ernie slurped energetically, then began to fish out the pasta alphabet. He arranged the limp letters on his napkin. 'Look,

I've almost got your name.' He addressed the rest of the family. 'Who's got an extra "O"?'

'Sorry, son,' George said. 'I've just eaten all my vowels.'

'Sarah?' Ernie asked.

'Forget it, Ernie,' Sarah said.

The Bigfoot raised the bowl and drank his soup in one great gurgle. Then he scooped up all the noodles in the bottom and offered them to Ernie. 'Thanks,' Ernie said. 'But you've squished them.'

The fact that Ernie and the Bigfoot were communicating wasn't lost on George. The creature was obviously intelligent. He learned fast. As George spooned his soup, an idea began to take shape. By the time he swallowed his last consonant, it was a full-blown scheme. Now all he had to do was find a way to spend some time alone with Bigfoot.

Luck was on his side. The phone rang. 'Look, Irene,' Nancy said into the phone, 'why don't I come over there? George isn't feeling well, and things are still a little crazy around here . . .' When she hung up, she looked apologetically at George. 'You don't mind, do you? I figured it was better to head her off at the pass.'

'Good thinking,' George said. 'You go ahead. And don't worry about a thing, Nan. I'll hold the fort.'

'You're looking kind of stressed, Nan,' Irene said. 'Why don't you try some of this?' She pointed to the frothy light-brown stuff in the blender. 'It'll make you feel like a million bucks.'

'Thanks,' Nancy said, 'but I've just eaten.'

'What?' Irene asked.

'What what?'

'What did you eat?'

'Alphabet soup.'

'Nancy, Nancy. I can't believe you feed your family that junk. It's full of chemicals.'

'George is allergic to brewer's yeast,' Nancy said. 'I'll just have a cup of coffee, if you don't mind.'

They settled at the kitchen table. Irene was full of questions. What was wrong with George? (Just a touch of indigestion.) How was their vacation? (Great, just great.) You kids didn't have a fight or anything, did you? (Who, us? We never fight.) Nancy finally found a way to stop the interrogation. She asked Irene to fill her in on all the latest developments in *General Hospital*.

It was a stroke of genius. Irene was off and running.

Two hours later Nancy managed to escape. Safe inside the kitchen, she leaned against the door and let out a long sigh. George was hard at work, trying to repair the doorway to the dining-room. He flashed her an eager grin. 'Ready to see something?'

'Give me a minute. Irene just ran one week of soaps by me. You'd think they were her relatives, the way she carries on. But I asked for it. It was better than the third degree. Oh, and she's invited us out tonight. Dinner and bowling.' Nancy smiled hopefully at Georgc. 'I said no. Told her you had something to drop off. Don't you?'

George gave her the cat-digesting-canary grin that reminded her of Ernie. 'Don't be so sure. You just might change your mind when you see this.'

'Where *is* our guest?' Nancy asked.

'Ernie's showing him the bathroom.'

Nancy was sorry she asked. She used to like their bathroom. George motioned her to follow him into the living-room. Sarah was engaged in a meaningful relationship with the telephone receiver. When she saw Nancy, she covered the mouthpiece. 'I feel like a prisoner, mom. Can I go out?'

George shook his head. 'No. You're at home, sick. Besides, I don't want you to miss this.'

'Sasha? My dad's being Attila the Hun. I can't go.'

Ernie and the creature emerged from the bathroom. Ernie shut the door carefully behind them. Nancy took it for a bad sign. Ernie never remembered to shut a door.

'How'd he do?' George asked.

Ernie's expression was not encouraging. 'C-minus, D-plus. I'd recommend using the upstairs john for the next couple of years.'

Nancy wanted to assess the damage. She headed for the bathroom, but Ernie stepped in front of the door. 'Trust me, mom. You've got your whole life ahead of you.'

Nancy was not so sure. She wanted to know the worst, but George was bouncing up and down like a carnival barker. 'Okay, okay everybody. Your attention, please. We . . .' – he pointed to the creature – 'have something to show you. But first I want you to think about this for a moment. Us. Life. Time.'

For a moment Nancy worried about George. It wasn't like him to turn philosophical in the middle of a family crisis. Sarah and Ernie stared blankly at their father. They weren't prepared to contemplate life's mysteries right then either.

George gaped back at them. 'Magazines. You know? Cover stories. I mean, you could be looking at old Dad here on TV, for heaven's sake. Okay, you'll see. Just watch.' With that, he reached in his pocket, brought out a sugar cube and held it up in front of Bigfoot. The creature went for it. George raised his hand, palm out, like a schoolboy patrol. The creature stopped dead.

George beamed at the family. 'We started with something simple, but I think you'll see there's no stopping him.' Again, George raised the sugar cube.

TILT. MISTAKE. All Nancy's warning lights were flashing. Still, when George looked at her to see if she was watching, he seemed so proud of himself, so eager to please, that Nancy tried to smile.

'Sit!' George commanded. 'Sit!'

The creature thought about it for a second or two. Then he sat. His method of sitting consisted of kicking his legs straight out in front and letting his butt fall where it would. In this case, it landed on the sofa. The sofa would never be the same again.

'That's great, dad!' Ernie was impressed. Sarah dropped the telephone. She looked as appalled as Nancy felt. George shrugged. The creature stood up and looked at the sagging couch.

'You taught him to sit!' Ernie enthused.

He'd said the magic word. The creature sat. He sat on the coffee table this time. The coffee table wasn't quite up to the excitement. It splintered like kindling into a sorry heap.

George raced into the kitchen and returned with a whole

box of sugar cubes. He offered them all to Bigfoot. 'Enough! Here! Don't sit.'

Either the creature wasn't quite fluent in English yet or he didn't hear the 'don't'. He sat on a lamp. It was Nancy's favourite lamp. She used to like the table it sat on too. Now both were pulverized. George looked as though he knew just how Frankenstein felt when his monster got out of hand. He raced up to the Bigfoot, begging, 'Stay! Stay!'

The Bigfoot stayed. Nancy thought he looked proud of himself. She might have laughed at the 'yes, master' look he gave George, if only she hadn't been so tempted to cry about her furniture.

Ernie was enthralled by the performance. 'That was outstanding, dad!' George winced at his son's praise.

Nancy turned to George. 'If I could have a word with you before the auditions start?' She motioned him towards the kitchen. George looked a little hang-dog as he followed her. Behind them, in the living-room, she could hear Sarah returning to her phone, while Ernie invited the Bigfoot to catch some cable TV.

When they were alone in the kitchen Nancy counted to ten, but it didn't help. She was still angry. George should have been glad she didn't yell at him in front of the kids. They'd agreed a long time ago to present a united front. Well, she'd kept her part of the bargain, but now, by God, she was going to let him have it.

'George Nathan Henderson! What on earth's the matter with you? This is our home! These are our things. George! You're acting like a crazy person.'

George seemed to know he had it coming. He took it well and answered quietly. 'That wasn't supposed to happen.'

Nancy was beyond apologies. She wanted action. 'This whole thing wasn't supposed to happen, but it did. And now we have to do the right thing.'

The right thing was obvious to her, but it seemed to elude George. 'I know it seems bad,' he said, 'but just give me a week.'

'George! We don't have enough house for two days. It doesn't fit here. And it doesn't fit in our lives. Now do the right thing. Think about *him.*' Nancy was just hitting her stride, about to get eloquent about the right thing. George would have to listen. She *was* right, and he must know it. No matter what crazy illusions of fame and fortune had temporarily misguided him, her husband was not a fool. Nancy hoped he was not a fool.

Ernie came sailing in in mid-lecture. 'Mom! Dad! Hurry! This is great.'

Nancy looked at George. He looked at her. In the face of impending disaster, they were back in the same team. Warily, they followed Ernie into the living-room.

In kingly fashion, the Bigfoot was reclining in a chair. His big feet hung over the end and rested on the sofa. His eyes were glued to the television screen. There, in living colour, a younger version of the President of the United States was conversing with a chimpanzee.

'It's called *Bedtime for Bonzo,*' Ernie said. 'He really likes the monkey.'

'He has good taste then,' Nancy said. 'The monkey is the better actor.'

'Now watch this,' Ernie said. He dipped a corn chip into the plastic tub of clam dip and popped it in his mouth. The Bigfoot plucked a yellow leaf from Nancy's ficus tree, dipped it and ate. 'Cool, huh!' Ernie said. 'He didn't care for the blue cheese.'

Ernie pointed to the living-room wall, where the contents of a pint of blue-cheese dip were slowly sliding down. As they watched the Roquefort ooze on to the carpet, Bigfoot leaned forward to cop another snack. The chair collapsed under him. Not quickly, not even noisily, but in a kind of graceful slow motion George's favourite chair, the chair from which he'd watched something like two million televised sporting events, gave up the ghost. For a moment the Bigfoot lay spraddled on his back like a giant furry beetle, then, rolling to his knees, he freed himself and settled, cross-legged, in front of the TV.

George's face looked as collapsed as the chair. Now that her point was made, Nancy felt sorry for him. She was sure his head had been full of beautiful dreams. With a surge of real affection, she put her arm around the big lug and kissed him. Poor dear George.

'Okay, you're right,' he said. 'I'll take him back. But this may not be so easy.'

Just then the Bigfoot laughed out loud. Nancy looked at the television in time to see Bonzo making a monkey out of the future President.

'I think he likes it here,' George said.

• Chapter Fourteen

Ernie promised himself he would never be a grown-up. Grown-ups were stupid. They did bad things. His grown-up mother and grown-up father were going to take the Bigfoot back to the woods. He tried and tried to talk some sense into them, but they hardly listened. All they did was give him those dumb grown-up smiles and pat his head. Ernie couldn't stand it. And his jerk of a sister was on their side. Of course, she was half grown-up herself. Much as he hated to admit it.

Ernie tried to keep the creature happy while they waited around for dark. They watched some more TV. They listened to records. Ernie showed the Bigfoot how to dance. Mom wouldn't let them go outside. Even after it was dark, they had to wait for Mrs Moffitt to leave for the bowling alley. Finally he heard her car start up.

His mom turned from the window. 'All clear. It's time, Ernie.'

Ernie gave it one last shot. 'How about if he stays in my room? I don't mind this kind of destruction.'

His mom's look told him she wasn't willing to negotiate. Ernie took the Bigfoot's big, warm hand in his and led him out through the kitchen on to the back porch. The car was ready and waiting.

Mom turned to the Bigfoot. 'You remember this, don't you? Your favourite station wagon. It's nicer inside.'

Her voice was all syrupy and reassuring, the same voice she used in the doctor's office just before the nurse would sink her needle in Ernie's arm. The Bigfoot was suspicious. He wasn't going near the car.

Ernie's dad crouched in front, trying to tie the bumper back on with baling wire. A mountain of junk food, the kind they usually didn't eat, sat on the bonnet. Mom nudged Ernie. He nudged the Bigfoot. Together they moved towards the car. As soon as the neighbourhood dog pack caught wind of the creature, they gathered at the fence. Dad looked up and gave the Bigfoot a phony smile. 'Hungry?' he said. 'We're . . . uh . . . we're going to have a little party.'

'Yeah,' Ernie said. 'A goodbye party.'

Now his dad gave *him* a phony smile. Ernie wasn't buying it.

The creature studied his dad's repair job. He leaned down and shook the bumper, then ripped it off the car. His dad gritted his teeth and smiled again. 'Ah, Plan B. No problem,' Dad said. Ernie wished his face would crack. It ought to be illegal to smile when you didn't really mean it.

The Bigfoot lifted up the bumper as if it was light as a chopstick (which, to him, it probably was) and sent it flying over the hedge. A few seconds later they heard the SPLASH. Without even looking, he'd hit the Moffitt's pool. 'See what we're going to be missing?' Ernie said.

His dad wiped his hands on his trousers. 'Well, let's eat. Nancy? Ern?' He turned to the Bigfoot. 'How about a burger?'

Ernie grabbed a fish sandwich from the pile on the car and passed a burger to his mom. Food always made him feel better. Dad unwrapped a burger and held it out to the Bigfoot. The Bigfoot took it, smelled it, then peeled off the top bun. Underneath the lettuce and tomato he found the hamburger. It didn't look too appetizing when he held it up between two of his big fingers – almost but not quite enough to spoil Ernie's appetite. Bigfoot's nose wrinkled as if he smelled something dead. He roared at the hamburger patty, then threw it to the pack of the dogs outside the fence. They dived for it.

'Right!' Dad said. 'Yours was the fish.'

He snatched the sandwich Ernie'd just opened and handed it to the creature. 'These are for him,' Dad said. 'The burgers are for you.'

There were a lot of burgers on the bonnet. Ernie felt his stomach lurch, especially after the burger autopsy the creature had just performed. Bigfoot liked fish better too. He finished off Ernie's sandwich in one swallow. Dad offered him another. Just as the Bigfoot reached out to take it, Dad started to back away around the side of the car. He opened the door and put the sandwich on the back seat. 'Come on,' he muttered, 'a tasty catch, smothered in tartare sauce . . .'

The creature started to follow, then wised up. Dad went for the fries. 'And french fries. Large! Two orders!' The french fries appealed to the Bigfoot's vegetarian appetite. He inched towards the car.

'And how about chocolate milk shake to wash those down, huh?'

That did it. Bigfoot followed Dad. Dad opened up the food bag and let him peek inside. Then he tossed it into the back seat. The Bigfoot climbed in after it. Maybe he thought it was another trick. As soon as he was inside the wagon, Dad climbed in front. Ernie heard the door locks click. Through the window, Ernie could see the Bigfoot try to sit up. The ceiling was a little low.

'Comfortable?' Dad asked.

The Bigfoot sat up. A huge metal blister rose from the roof of the station wagon as the creature customized it with his head. Now he could sit up straight. He grinned at Ernie.

'That's the thing about these old beauties,' Dad said. 'Plenty of head room.'

It wasn't funny. Not at all. Ernie wasn't sure he would have felt worse if his dad was taking his mom to live in the woods. If it were Sarah, he wouldn't shed a tear. But it tore him apart to see the Bigfoot in the back seat and to know he'd never see him again. Ernie ran into the house so the Bigfoot wouldn't see him crying. He heard Mom come in after him. Sarah was still talking on the telephone to her dumb friend Sasha. Girls had no feelings at all.

Ernie was taking it hard. George sighed. He could not drive off with his son in tears. George climbed out of the car and locked the doors. To the Bigfoot, looking puzzled in the back seat, he said, 'Just . . .' – he caught himself before he uttered 'sit' – 'you just stay right here.'

Sarah and her pet telephone were in the doorway. When George hurried past her, she dropped the receiver long enough to say, 'You're not changing your mind, are you?'

George didn't stop to answer. In the kitchen Nancy had her arm around Ernie. She was doing her best to explain why an eight-foot Sasquatch wouldn't flourish in the suburbs. Her arguments were sound and sensible, but they didn't seem to be having much impact on their son. Ernie's shoulders were rounded sadly, and George could hear him sniffing back his tears. George put his hands on his son's shoulders and turned him round. Ernie's eyes were red and disappointed. George knelt beside him, hoping he could find the right words to explain, to comfort.

'Mom's right, Ernie. I know this is hard. It's hard for me, too, but it's the right thing to do. I was wrong to think we could just claim him as ours, like some kind of stray dog. He's a man. You were the first to see it. He deserves to be free. So what do you say we go out there like a couple of men and say, "Goodbye, hairy . . ."'

George meant to say 'hairy friend', but before he got the last word out, a bone-shattering thud sounded in the driveway. Ernie looked quizzical. *'Harry?* Since when has he had a name?'

'Since now,' George said.

They all, even Sarah, went outside to see what had made the noise. The door lay on the ground and the car was empty. As the family stared at the car, they could hear two dozen dogs running off into the night, yipping, their toenails clicking against the pavement.

A moment later, above the canine howls, there rose a long and mournful wail that could only have come from Harry.

'That's him!' Ernie said what they all were thinking. 'He doesn't sound too happy.'

George put his hand on Ernie's shoulder. 'No, son, he doesn't.'

'Why did he run away, dad?'

'I'm not sure, son. But I think he understands more than we realized. I think he didn't want to cause us trouble.'

'What now?' Nancy said. 'We can't just let him go wandering around the city streets. He's innocent as a baby, George. And there are lots of creeps out there.'

Slowly, George nodded. He looked at the remains of his

recently classic car, then fished for the keys in his pocket. 'I'd better go and look for him,' he said.

'Can I come, too, dad?' Ernie asked.

'No, son,' George said. He watched Ernie's face fall and thought as fast as he could. 'I need you to wait here with Mom and Sarah. In case he comes back.'

That seemed to satisfy Ernie. George climbed into his disintegrating station wagon and set off in search of Bigfoot.

• Chapter Fifteen

It had taken Harry a while to understand that the male was full-grown. He was so small. But the other members of his group treated him with respect. The female with the shining hair was full-grown too. She was the mate of the male, the mother of the others. The young male who played with him and the young female who growled at him were immature. Together they made a family. There were no elders.

Harry wondered when he would see his mate again. He missed his children.

Still, these creatures were kind to him. The female nursed his hand and gave him food. The young male shared his tools and toys. These creatures had wonderful toys. The male played with him too – the Food Game. The male offered Harry food and asked him to do something. When Harry did it, the male gave him the food. Harry did not understand why the male wanted him to sit down – it was so simple – but he liked the little pieces of sweet white food the male gave him when he sat. He knew of nothing quite so sweet in the forest.

None of his kind had ever left the forest. Legend told of other two-legged creatures on the earth, but few had ever seen them. The young ones were warned to keep hidden from them. The elders said they were cruel. They killed and ate other animals. They ate their own dead.

Perhaps the elders were wrong. True, these creatures hung parts of dead animals on the walls of their cave, but Harry did not believe they ate their own kind. The female grew many kinds of plants. He liked the taste of her flowers. When he returned to the forest, Harry would tell the elders about these creatures and their ways. He wondered if they would believe him. Already Harry had seen many winters. One day he would be an elder himself. It made him smile to think he would be called 'the One Who Left the Forest'.

Harry did not understand why he had been chosen for this adventure. He was not sure how he would get back to the forest. But it encouraged him that the creatures seemed to be intelligent. More and more he was able to communicate with them. When the time was right, when he had learned more of their language or they had learned more of his, he would ask them to help him return to his home.

Darkness came. The creatures lighted their cave. Harry was hungry and wondered when they would give him food. The young male took his hand and led him outside the cave. The male knelt beside the thing they called 'car'. Inside it the creatures could move as fast as Harry could run. The car was broken. Harry helped the male to fix it.

The male offered him food. The food did not smell good. Harry threw it away. The male gave him better food. Harry understood they were playing a game. The male put the food in the car. Harry got into the car. He ate the food. The male got into the car.

Through the hole in the side of the car Harry saw the young male begin to cry. He saw sadness on the face of the female. The child and the female returned to the cave. The male made an unhappy sound. He got out of the car but told Harry to stay inside it.

Through the entrance to their cave Harry watched the creatures and saw they were unhappy. He did not know how, but he knew it was he who had made them unhappy. This made him unhappy too. He did not wish to hurt them.

If he went away, perhaps they would be happy again. He did not want to go away. This place was strange to him. He had no way of knowing if all the creatures were as kind as these. He did not know how he would find his way home. But he knew he must leave.

Harry tried to open the door as he had seen the male do, but it would not open. Inside the cave the female held the young male while he wept. Harry pushed against the door until it gave way and climbed out of the car. He stepped into the shadows. A pack of four-legged animals that reminded him of wolves, or of coyotes, came yapping after him. Fast as he could, Harry ran into the night.

Soon Harry had outrun the yapping creatures. He ran on and on for a long time. The stars came out. As the night wore on, the place became quieter. There were fewer people and fewer cars. Harry ran for a long time. When he stopped to get his bearings, he did not believe he was any closer to the forest than he had been before. And he was hungry. The food the creatures gave him did not fill him up for long.

Around him there were many caves. He picked one that reminded him of the cave of his friends. He watched and listened. The creatures who lived there must be gone or sleeping. He crept closer and looked inside. There was a food box like the one in the cave of his friends. As quietly as he could, Harry let himself into the cave and crept up to the food box. He opened it and began to explore inside. He sampled the food. Some of it fell out on to the floor. By accident, he broke the light inside the food box. In the darkness he found more food.

Harry was so hungry and so busy eating that he did not hear footsteps or see the light until it shone on his foot. He stepped backwards, out of the light, and tried to hide himself. He was afraid. The light went out. Harry waited.

All of a sudden the light flashed on again. A female creature sprang at him. She hit his foot. It scared more than hurt him. Harry growled at the female. The female closed her eyes and fell at Harry's feet. She did not move.

Harry reached down and poked at the female. Still she did not move. She was dead. He had not touched the creature, but he had killed her. It was forbidden among his kind to kill another living animal. He had meant the creature no harm. Harry knelt beside her and wept.

Among his own kind it was important to honour the dead. Harry wished to honour the dead creature, but he was not sure how. His kind buried their dead deep in the earth. He thought about burying the female. Then he remembered the male deer he had found on the wall of his friends' cave. Was that their way? He studied the dead creature.

Then he remembered. When the creatures thought he was dead, they had laid him on top of their car. The more he thought about it, the more it made sense. The creatures were very fond of their cars. He did not doubt they had some legend to explain it. Harry smiled, pleased that he understood their custom.

Through the door to the cave he saw a car outside. Gently he lifted the dead creature in his arms and carried her out of the cave. Carefully he laid her body on top of the car. He folded her arms across her chest. The creature looked as if she were asleep. Harry was sorry she was dead. He honoured her.

• Chapter Sixteen

When Ernie woke up, Little Bob was snuggled warmly against his back. Obnoxious music from the local early morning TV show blared up the stairs. The TV in the kitchen was like the family alarm clock. At night his mom set the timer and turned the volume up full-blast. Ernie shook Little Bob awake, then scuffled with him.

'We were going to take Harry back to the woods last night,' Ernie told the dog, 'but he ran away. That's what dad named him – Harry. It kind of fits, don't you think?'

Little Bob climbed on Ernie's chest and licked his face. Mrs Moffitt probably hadn't given him enough attention when they were gone. Ernie wouldn't have been surprised if she'd forgotten to feed him too. He closed both hands around Little Bob's ribcage and lifted him high above the bed. 'Zoom. It's Super Dog.' Bob clawed at the air, and Ernie let him down. The dog settled back down in his nest in Ernie's blankets.

'Say, Bob,' Ernie said, 'you're an animal. Do you think you'd rather live in the woods than in a house?'

With a contented growl, Little Bob snuggled deeper in the covers.

'I mean, you're a wild thing, too, aren't you? Just think, you could spend your time catching rabbits and squirrels instead of waiting around for us to give you tinned food.' The more he thought about it, the more that sounded right to Ernie. Civilization wasn't good for animals. It was unnatural. When Ernie's third-grade class had won the paper chase, the reward was a movie, *Born Free*, about a lioness. It made a deep impression on Ernie, so deep he could still whistle the theme music from memory. The more he thought about it, the clearer it became to him. Ernie climbed out of bed and snatched up Little Bob.

Luckily, the rest of the family was in the kitchen when he got downstairs. Ernie opened the front door as quietly as he could and put Little Bob out on the mat. 'You're free, Little Bob,' he told the dog. 'Go back to the wild. Run free.'

Little Bob looked up at Ernie. He was used to company on his morning walk. 'Go on, Bob,' Ernie said. He shooed the dog towards the street and tried to feel as sad as his dad looked last night when they let the Bigfoot go. Little Bob trotted off, and Ernie shut the door. With the sleeve of his pyjamas, he wiped away the one tear he'd managed to squeeze out before he went into the kitchen to see what was for breakfast.

The Alaska Airlines commercial was just ending. The morning show came on. 'And now, your host, the toast of the Olympic coast, Jerry Seville!' The kitchen filled up with the sound of fake clapping. Ernie's mom was making everybody's lunch. His dad came in from the downstairs bathroom, shaved and dressed for work. Even over the coffee, Ernie could smell his aftershave. Old Spice. Ernie was going to wear the same kind when he was old enough to shave. Ernie's mom handed his dad a cup of coffee.

'God, I hate this guy,' his dad said.

His mom said, 'I'll change it.'

'No, let me hate him. It'll keep me awake until the coffee kicks in.'

Ernie looked closely at his dad. His eyes were kind of red and puffy. Dad had spent half the night driving around looking for Harry. Mom made Ernie go to bed before he got home. She promised to wake him up if Dad found Harry.

The guy his dad hated on TV was saying how glad he was it was already Tuesday. 'Go to hell, Jerry,' Ernie's dad said back. Ernie laughed, but not too loudly. He didn't want to discourage his father from saying what he really felt.

Ernie opened the refrigerator door, looking for some juice or maybe milk. Pickles, ketchup, mustard, a couple of cans of beer. The fridge was as empty as Ernie ever remembered seeing it. 'Hey, mom, what are we supposed to eat for breakfast around here?' he asked.

His mother shushed him. 'Listen.'

Ernie stared at the television. The announcer, the one his dad hated, was reading from the newspaper.

'Last night a Hawthorne Hills man reported that he found his wife lying unconscious on the roof of their car . . .' The announcer looked up from the paper and snickered. 'When the woman was revived by paramedics, she said she must have been put there by the huge, hairy, manlike creature resembling the legendary Bigfoot that she had earlier mistaken for a mouse.' The announcer laughed his head off.

Dad sat back down at the table. 'Harry!'

'He went to the Hills?' Mom said.

'Come on,' the announcer guy said. 'Bigfoot?! We go through this every couple of years, for crying out loud!'

Dad stood up. He started to take off his tie. 'I can't go to work. I've got to find him.'

'George,' Mom said, 'he wouldn't have left if he didn't want to. Let him go. Go to work!'

It was pretty clear to Ernie that the announcer didn't believe there was such a thing as Bigfoot. Ernie could understand why his dad couldn't stand the guy. Dad was staring at the television with a glazed look. Mom waved her hand in front of his face. 'Earth to George. It's time to go to work. Now. Mush.'

Slowly Ernie's dad snugged up the knot on his tie and kissed his mom goodbye. Ernie looked away. He hated kissing. His dad left. The television cycled on to another commercial. His mother turned to him and Sarah. 'All right, guys, let's get a move on. What'll it be? Cereal? Eggs? Juice?'

'Uh, mom, have you looked in the refrigerator lately?' Ernie asked.

'Oh, right,' his mom said. 'How about some toast and a nice glass of water? Speciality of the house.'

Just then Ernie heard a familiar scratching sound at the back door. When he opened the door, Little Bob came bouncing in. Ernie was glad to see him, he had to admit. He crouched down and held out his arms. Little Bob jumped in. Ernie gave him a welcome-home squeeze. 'You came back, Little Bob. Hey, mom. He came back.'

His mother gave him one of her that's-nice-dear smiles. She

probably thought Little Bob had just been outside for the usual reason. Ernie shrugged and sat down to his toast and water. It wasn't much of a way to start a school day. His mom noticed him gagging down the dry toast and grinned at him. 'Don't worry, Ernie. I'll make it to Safeway before supper time.'

All the time he was getting dressed and walking to school, Ernie debated whether or not to say anything to the other kids about the Bigfoot. Everybody was going to know why he was a day late. For now, he decided, he'd tell them they'd had an accident on the way home from camping. Then, if the picture he took turned out, maybe he'd come across with the whole story. Meanwhile, he swore himself to secrecy. He didn't want to get laughed at this early in the year.

Sarah was worried about her hair. Nancy assured her it looked fine. Sarah studied herself in the glass front of the microwave. 'No, it doesn't, mom. It looks like I washed it in the sprinkler.'

Nancy gave her daughter a hug. 'No one will ever know. You better get going or you'll miss the bus.'

With one last glance at her reflection, Sarah grabbed her notebooks and headed out. Nancy cleared the table, turned off the television set and sat down to enjoy her second cup of coffee. It was still too early to call the plumber or the contractor to come and repair the damage. She kicked off her slippers and put her feet up on the empty chair across the way. Peace. She deserved it.

No sooner had Nancy turned her attention to the crossword puzzle in the morning paper than she heard a sharp knock on the kitchen door. No mistaking that sound. Irene had arrived.

So much for peace. If anything ever drove Nancy back into the work force, it would be Irene. Nancy felt sorry for her, but that didn't make her daily visits any easier to take. Nancy sometimes wondered what it must be like at Irene's house to make the Hendersons' home so appealing.

Irene let herself in, as usual. 'Morning, neighbour. Gee, I'm glad you guys are back. Not that Little Bob's bad company. He just doesn't talk much, you know.'

Nancy nodded while Irene helped herself to coffee and sat down at the kitchen table. 'Say, you read the paper yet? Seems

Bigfoot's back in the news. Jeez, when are people going to grow up?'

'I'm a grown-up and I like Bigfoot stories,' Nancy said.

'Yeah, he's right up there with Santa and the Easter Bunny.' Irene blew on her coffee. 'You know, there's supposed to be some old hunter out there who's spent his whole life trying to catch one. Isn't that the silliest thing you ever heard?'

Nancy nodded agreement. Just then the phone rang. Nancy went to answer it. As soon as she picked up the receiver a sharp knock sounded on the door. Irene heaved herself up from the table and went to answer it.

The man on the front porch didn't look as though he lived in the neighbourhood. Actually, he looked kind of like an over-the-hill Marlboro Man, all tan and weathered. He wasn't exactly dressed for downtown. Irene stopped staring and remembered her manners. 'Can I help you?' she asked.

The man opened a leather bag and pulled out a car's number plate. 'Quite possibly,' he said, 'we can help each other. I believe this is yours.'

Irene knew very well that the number plate was not hers. She shoved it back at the stranger. 'What are you sellin', buster?'

Nancy hung up the phone – it was a wrong number – and joined Irene at the door. The man outside was well past middle age and looked as if he belonged in the woods. When he spoke Nancy thought she heard the trace of an accent in his gruff voice. 'Mrs Henderson?'

Nancy was surprised the stranger knew her name. She was even more surprised when he handed her a battered number plate. She recognized the number. It was theirs. The man's look questioned her. She turned to Irene. 'Say, would you go turn off the kettle? I left it on high.'

'I'm Richard Smith, U S Forestry Service. We're investigating a possible road kill . . . an animal killed or maimed in an auto accident.'

Nancy wished George were at home. They hadn't discussed what to do if anyone found out. She decided to play dumb.

'You did hit something on Route A 4? A small logging road?' Even as he spoke, the man tried to see around her into the house. Nancy had the uneasy feeling that he was sniffing the air. Had the air freshener done its work?

'Yes, we did hit something.'

'What was it, Mrs Henderson?'

'I don't know,' Nancy said. 'I mean, it was fast, we couldn't really see.'

'Where is it now?'

The man hammered away, just like a TV detective. His persistence rattled Nancy. 'Now? It . . . whatever it was ran away.' She had the feeling the Forest Service man knew she wasn't exactly telling the whole truth. His voice was stern. 'Mrs Henderson. Our main concern is for the safety of your family. To be sure no one was injured.'

'Oh, no. No one was injured.'

'But we're also deeply concerned for the well-being of the animal. If it's out there suffering, well, surely you'd want to help us find it and take care of it?'

'Surely,' Nancy said. 'But it's okay. It just walked into the woods. Didn't even limp.'

The stranger raised his eyebrows. 'It walked?'

'Ah, you know . . . ran. Ah, waddled. Scurried. Scrambled. Crawled. Like animals do. But we're okay, and I'm sure it's okay.'

This time she was sure the visitor was sniffing the air. Nancy took a deep sniff herself. Maybe the house still did smell a little weird. 'Oh, Jeez, I almost forgot. I've got a sink backed up in here. The toilet too. Gotta go now. Bye.' She slammed the door shut and leaned against it.

Irene appeared. She carried a steaming mug. 'I made you a cup of tea.'

'Oh, thanks, Irene.'

'Number plate. The guy's probably a convict. What you don't need right now is somebody bothering you. Just sit down and try to relax.'

For once Nancy kind of appreciated Irene's company. She took her tea mug and looked for a place to sit down and enjoy it. The living-room was out of the question. It looked as though a vicious and very localized tornado had just blown through. Irene surveyed the rubble, then gave Nancy a sympathetic smile. 'I remember Herb's and my first fight,' she said.

Nancy curbed the impulse to say she and George never fought. She smiled weakly at Irene. 'Why don't you come in the kitchen and tell me all about it?' She settled back to hear the gory details. It wasn't as if she was prying. Irene was going to tell her whether she wanted to hear or not. Irene was like that.

• Chapter Seventeen

All the way to work George worried about Harry. The car was still full of his pungent scent. It also looked awful. George wasn't ready for any smart remarks about his missing bumper or the homemade sunroof. He pulled into the very last slot in the employees-only section of the car park.

Inside, the store was depressingly the same as when he'd left for his vacation, two Fridays before. Billers, from Fishing, and Stuart, from Fitness, were gathered around the Bunn Automatic Coffeemaker in the back room. George looked around for his favourite cup. There was a week's worth of dust inside. He wiped it out with the end of his tie.

'How about you, Henderson?' Stuart said. 'You see any Bigfoot?'

George couldn't hide his surprise. 'What?'

'Bigfoot,' Stuart said. 'You know, on your vacation.'

Whew. Safe. George managed a smile. Gone a week and he'd forgotten how to kid with the kidders. He shook his head, no. He didn't really want more coffee, but he poured it anyway. It was hard enough being the boss's son. Sometimes it was even harder to be one of the boys.

Billers picked up the Bigfoot stuff. 'I read that the things weigh over four hundred pounds and have a really bad smell.'

Stuart, the store funny man, lifted up his nose and started sniffing the air. 'Well, gee. Looks like we got one right here. What's your shoe size, Billers?'

'Very funny!' Billers said. Maybe he thought it was, though, because he started laughing. George figured he should laugh too, but he didn't think it was funny at all. He nodded to the guys and wandered off to his department. On his way he sniffed his shoulders, his shirt sleeves, then his hands. If the car still smelled of Bigfoot, maybe he did too.

George had just taken up his post in the Hunting Department when they unlocked the front door. Two seconds later a short, stocky guy strode in. He was as bald as a billiard ball and deeply tanned. Briefly, he scanned the store, then focused on George in Hunting.

'Can I help you?' George inquired.

'Probably not. You carry .458 Magnum rounds?'

George turned to the boxes of ammunition on the shelves behind him. 'We don't get much call for these monsters . . . Ah, here we are.' He put the box of cartridges on the counter.

Instead of being happy that George had them, the customer was angry. 'Criminy! This is the fourth place I've been to. Got any more?'

Just to be sure, George looked again. 'Sorry. That's it. You going on safari?'

'Son,' the guy told him, 'the really big game is American-grown.'

As far as George knew, there were no elephants native to North America. The Ice Age was supposed to have wiped out the mastodons. But, as his father insisted, the customer is always right. He nodded. 'That will be ten ninety-five.'

The big-game hunter didn't wait for his change, and apparently he didn't need a bag. He shoved the ammo into his coat pocket and hightailed it out of the store. As soon as he was gone, George's dad appeared on the floor. He looked tall, lean, tough, like a real sportsman. George was always impressed when he hadn't seen his father for a while. The old man really looked the part. He came over and leaned on the hunting counter. 'Jacques LaFleur. Like clockwork.'

George, who was never very talkative in his father's presence, said, 'Uhm?'

'He's always the first to show whenever these crazy sightings start up.'

'He bought some pretty serious ammo . . . 458s,' George said.

His father shook his head. 'Before this Sasquatch thing got

under his skin, he was a Class A hunter. Where do you think Claws came from?'

Claws was the biggest grizzly bear George had ever seen. For years, stuffed, it had stood guard at the entrance to his father's store. It was a nice touch, George had to admit. It scared little kids and women and made the male customers feel macho. Beyond Claws George saw the hunter climbing into a power wagon parked in front of the store. 'That guy shot Claws? Why would he part with a trophy like that?'

His dad said, 'Probably because it was the smallest one.'

George tightened his grip on the counter. What if he'd just sold the bullets that would kill Harry?

With admiration George's father watched the hunter depart. Then he looked back to George. 'He may be crazy, but he's a real man.'

'I bet,' George said.

During his lunch hour George hot-footed it to the library. He hadn't actually been inside it since he graduated from high school. To save himself time he consulted the bespectacled librarian at the information desk. 'Hi. This is my lunch break and I'm in kind of a hurry. Could you please point me towards some books on the Sasquatch? Bigfoot. You know.'

Without looking up from her computer terminal, the librarian said, 'Fantasy, Folk Lore, Myths and Legends. Fourth floor, at the very back of the library.'

George nodded thanks. 'You can also try Children's Books,' the librarian called after him. George bolted up the stairs. The library was bigger than he remembered, with reading rooms fanning out north, south, east and west from a central lobby on each floor. On the fourth floor he circled the compass, then decided on east for anthropology. Students bent over books at the long tables, and in the easy chairs, sometimes with books for props, sometimes without them, old men dozed. When he found his section George looked around for the card catalogue, only to find that since his school years they'd put the whole thing on microfiche. When he had finally figured out how to use the viewer and found his categories, he copied down the numbers and headed for the shelves. Seventeen minutes of his lunch hour were already gone.

The selection wasn't the best. All of the books had a small-time, unofficial look to them, as if they'd been published by Crackpot Press in somebody's basement. George scanned indexes – B for Bigfoot, S for Sasquatch – and filled his arms with everything that looked as if it might possibly be useful.

The librarian who checked out his stack gave George a gentle smile. 'Nobody's taken these out since the last time there was a sighting. See?' She pointed to the stamped date on the card. 'Nineteen eighty-one. I think that's the time the *National Inquirer* ran a front-page story called "I Was Bigfoot's Love Slave". We had to put the books on reserve for a while.'

'Yeah, right,' George said. 'Actually, these are for my son. He's doing a term paper.' George thought the librarian knew he was lying. He grabbed the books and ran.

That night, after supper, George and Ernie settled down to study the Bigfoot books. The first one they picked up featured pictures of Sasquatch looking meaner and weirder than Frankenstein's pet monster. Over George's shoulder, Ernie exclaimed, 'This book stinks.'

Nancy automatically protested about her son's choice of words.

'These pictures don't look at all like Harry,' Ernie said.

George looked up. 'He's right, Nan. No wonder people want to kill them. The accounts in here, the pictures, they make Bigfoot out to be a killer.' Nancy sat down beside him to check out the pictures as he flipped through. Near the back he hit upon a picture of Jacques LaFleur. Nancy pointed at the page. 'Hey, that's him.'

'That's LaFleur, the hunter who bagged Claws.'

'It can't be.'

'Yeah. He was in the store today.'

'No,' Nancy insisted. 'His name is Smith, the Forestry guy I told you about. He was here at the house.'

A terrible look crossed Nancy's face just as a terrible thought crossed George's mind. 'That lying slime!' she said.

Both kids turned to stare at their mother. She never talked

like that. It got them sent to bed. When they were up the stairs, Nancy put her hand on George's shoulder. 'Come on to bed now, George. You need some rest.'

George put his hand over Nan's and squeezed. 'I'll be up in a minute. I just want to finish this first. It's the only one that's halfway accurate.'

Nancy said goodnight and went upstairs. George flipped through the pages. He found another picture of Jacques LaFleur, grinning beside some plaster castings of Bigfoot prints. LaFleur looked a lot younger in the picture. He had more hair. George turned to the copyright page: 1956. No wonder. The guy had been hunting Bigfoot for more than thirty years. George prayed that LaFleur's dedication was greater than his luck.

'Take care of yourself, Harry,' he said out loud.

• Chapter Eighteen

As long as it was dark Harry kept moving. Just past dawn the streets began to fill with cars. Harry remembered the warnings of the elders. Even if the creatures were not dangerous to him, he might be dangerous to them. Harry did not want to cause more deaths.

He found a small, green place that reminded him of the forest, helped himself to a meal of leaves and flowers, hid carefully in the bushes and settled down to sleep.

When Harry woke it was near dark. No creatures were about. His stomach was empty. Again he fed on the edible plants, then set out on his journey. The creatures lit their streets. Harry moved in and out of shadows.

Soon his instinct told him he was being hunted. Harry was not afraid. The creatures were poor hunters. Their noses and their ears were weak compared with his, and he had learned from childhood how to avoid them. All night they searched and Harry stayed ahead of them. It was as easy as a children's game.

Once, in the spirit of play, he let them catch a glimpse of him. He heard their voices rise, calling to one another. He heard their footsteps, running to where they thought he was. But Harry was not there any more. He was an expert at the hiding game.

• Chapter Nineteen

Nancy pulled on her favourite flannel nightgown and sat down on the edge of the bed. She was looking forward to a good night's sleep. Just as she was about to crawl under the covers, there was a soft knock on the door. Sarah stuck her head into the bedroom.

'Mom, could I talk to you for a minute?'

'Sure.' Nancy patted the bed beside her.

'Mom, I know you're awfully busy trying to repair the house and everything, but you did promise you'd take me shopping. I was wondering if we could make it tomorrow after school.'

Nancy sighed. She used to enjoy shopping with her daughter. That was back in the days when Sarah could still make up her mind. Now it took her forty-five minutes just to pick out a pair of tights. 'What's so important it won't wait until the weekend?' she asked.

'I'm the only girl in the class without a big pink shirt,' Sarah said.

Nancy said, 'Great. Who wants to look like everybody else?'

'I do,' Sarah said.

'Look, honey, you've only been back to school one day. What if tomorrow everybody's wearing yellow?'

'They won't be. Pink is definitely big this year. I've talked it all over with Sasha.'

'Is that what took you an hour and a half on the phone tonight? I thought you were doing your homework.'

'We did some homework too. But, mom, there's more to high school than studying. These are supposed to be the best years of my life, and I intend to make the most of them.'

'I thought college was supposed to be the best years of your life.'

'I'm not taking any chances,' Sarah said. 'There might be a nuclear war before I get to college. Will you take me to Southcenter tomorrow, mom?'

Nancy put her arm around Sarah's shoulders. 'The way things have been going around here lately, I'm not planning anything more than five minutes in advance.'

'Does that mean yes?'

'It means we'll see. You get on to bed now. It's after ten o'clock.'

Sarah stood up and headed for the door.

'And don't forget to brush your teeth.'

'Mom, I'm not a baby any more.'

'I've noticed,' Nancy said. 'Goodnight.'

''Night, mom.'

Nancy climbed under the covers. To lie down felt delicious. She punched her pillow into the right shape for sleeping and leaned over to turn off the light. George padded into the room in his stockinged feet. 'Finish your research?' Nancy asked.

'It isn't really research,' George told her. 'Most of those things are comic books. Godzilla meets Jane Fonda in the western woods.' He sat down on the edge of the bed. 'I did find one lead, though. There's somebody called Wallace Wrightwood, Ph.D., who might know what he's talking about. He's got an anthropological institute or something not too far from the National Forest. I might drive up there after work tomorrow afternoon and check him out.'

'Oh, do,' Nancy said. 'Then I won't have to take Sarah to Southcenter.'

'Didn't you take her shopping before we went on vacation?'

'I did,' Nancy said. 'I did. But it seems everyone in high school is wearing this one particular kind of shirt. Sarah isn't going to rest until she has one too.'

'I thought she was saving for college,' George said.

'That was last week. This week it's live for today. Seems she's afraid the world might blow up before she gets to college.'

George unbuttoned his shirt. 'Kids,' he said. 'Were we ever that silly, Nan?'

Nancy smiled at him. 'Yes, George. We were.' She lay back

down on her pre-punched pillow. George stood up to take off his trousers. He hung them over the back of a chair, then went to the dresser for clean pyjamas. When he opened the drawer, he let out an 'eeek'.

'There's an animal in here, Nan, and it isn't Little Bob.'

Alarmed, Nancy sat up again. Then she remembered. 'Relax, George. It's just mother's stole. I hid it.'

George pulled the furs out of his pyjama drawer and held them up. 'I never did like this thing.' Wiggling the furs, he turned to Nancy. 'I mean, come on. Does this look like one of the finer things in life?'

It was an old joke, but Nancy laughed. Mother thought her only daughter should have married a doctor, or at least an orthodontist, not a sporting goods salesman. 'Well,' she said, 'Mother would never forgive me if her precious little critters ended up six feet deep.'

'Do me a favour and keep 'em on your side.' George laid the stole on top of the dresser. Suited up for sleep, he crawled into bed. 'I'm exhausted. What a day. I'm going to sleep like a log tonight for sure.'

'Be sure to stay away from chainsaws, then,' Nancy said. 'Goodnight.'

But George couldn't sleep. He lay on his back and watched the patterns of moonlight on the ceiling. Beside him, Nan turned over every thirty seconds or so. Finally, he said, 'Honey, can't you sleep?'

'Uh uh.'

'What are you thinking about?'

'Nothing,' Nancy told him. 'Garden of Eden. Mr Darwin. Stuff like that.'

George stared at the ceiling. 'Harry. He's amazing. If he's hungry, he eats. If he's thirsty, he drinks. Don't worry about him. He can take care of himself.'

'If he's curious, he takes out a wall.' Nancy was silent for a moment, watching the light show on the ceiling. 'George, we're so lucky. We have each other. And Sarah and Ernie. But Harry, he's out there all alone.'

'He's all right,' George said. 'He's survived all these years.'

Nancy turned to her side so she could see George in the

darkness. 'People have seen him. They are going to go hunt him down and try to kill him.'

George had an answer for that too. 'There've been a zillion sightings and nobody has ever killed one. Besides, all the people who say they've seen one are usually kooks or crazies. Except for our family, or course.'

Nancy couldn't tell if George was trying to reassure her or himself. 'Oh, George, do you think Harry's a family man?'

'Thing, sweetheart,' George corrected.

'What if he's a family thing? What if there's a cave somewhere full of little Bigfoots –'

'Little Bigfeet.'

'– little Bigfeet waiting for Big Bigfoot to come home? Only he might not make it.'

'Well, I'm sure Mrs Bigfoot will take care of them, sweetheart.'

The very thought brought tears to Nancy's eyes. 'Oh, George! Mrs Bigfoot!'

George put his arm around her and held her while she cried.

In his bedroom down the hall Ernie shared his pillow with Little Bob. 'What do you think, boy?' he said. 'Do you think that Bigfoot will make it back home?'

Little Bob didn't answer. Instead he licked Ernie's chin. Ernic wiped the dog slobber from his chin. 'Jeez, Bob, I wish you'd learn to brush your teeth,' he said.

• Chapter Twenty

Work. George was starting to hate going to work. It was just five minutes till opening when he arrived. Fortunately, his father didn't see him come in late. A bunch of the guys were lounging against the display cases in the hunting department, while Stuart read out loud from the morning paper. George found the keys in his pocket and knelt down to unlock the gun displays.

'"One said . . . ,"' Stuart stopped to chuckle to himself. 'Now get this, "It must have been the large, hairy giant he saw running from the scene."'

The guys joined Stuart in a big guffaw. George kept his face averted. He straightened the row of silencers inside the case and looked towards the doors. They weren't open yet, but a crowd was growing fast outside. Waiting customers spilled off the sidewalk into the street. When George's father approached the gun counter, doing his best Teddy Roosevelt stride, the rest of the guys scattered to their stations.

'Look at that, would you, son?' George's dad said. 'It's starting already.'

'We having a sale?'

'No.' His dad chuckled. 'It's these Bigfoot sightings. Brings 'em out of the woodwork. Everybody and his brother wants to load up and get into the act. Real shot in the arm for Seattle Sport and Game.' His dad turned a greedy grin on the horde of customers outside. They might be fools, but he was more than willing to take their money. Then he turned to George. 'Say, do you still fool around with that painting stuff?'

It was the first time his father had mentioned George's hobby since he refused to pay for art school. Maybe the old boy was coming around. 'Yeah,' George said. 'In fact, I've just been . . .'

'Good.' His father never had been one to let somebody else finish a sentence. 'Maybe you could save your old man a few bucks. How about drawing up a full-size Bigfoot? We'll put it in the window next to the gun section. Make him look real big and scary, you know, just as they're supposed to look, George. Hands in the air, claws out. Big fangs, a lot of drool . . .'

He should have known better, George told himself. He should have known.

'Let's put up a map of the area,' his dad went on, 'and we'll mark all the spots where people say they've seen this thing.' His dad stared into space, envisioning the glory of it all. 'This'll become kind of a Bigfoot Central. A BHQ.

The old man might have gone even further – sweatshirts, rewards – except that George interrupted him. 'Don't you think we might be encouraging a lot of unqualified people to go out running around with loaded weapons?'

His father gave him one of his best grow-up-and-get-with-the-programme looks. 'Come on. You know as well as I do there's nothing out there to shoot at.' The old man glanced again at the crowd of would-be killers outside. 'We're going to do more business today than Christmas Eve. And George. I want to keep an eye on the stock. If we start running low on anything, get on that phone and re-order. Tell 'em to put a rush on it.'

'Right,' George said.

His father looked at his watch, the super sport model that came with a built-in compass and barometer and was water-resistant up to four hundred feet. 'Nine-oh-five, son. Let's not keep the good people waiting any more. Get out there and SELL GUNS.'

It was one of those mornings George regretted being manager. Keys in hand, he headed for the front door. The crazies on the pavement watched him closely. When he opened up the store, they nearly trampled him.

George wondered now why he'd spent all that time teaching Harry to sit when a few lessons in urban guerrilla tactics would have been more useful.

• Chapter Twenty-one

George had come looking for science. What he found was rubbish. The North American Anthropological Institute had rip-off written all over it. It was the kind of building that just sort of grows over the years – a hunk of plywood here, a sheet of tarpaper there, with some long-gone relative's caravan incorporated into the overall design. The only thing missing was the fleet of dead cars in the yard. In their place there were signs, big, loud tacky signs, proclaiming 'THE TRUTH ABOUT BIGFOOT – AUTHENTIC SOUVENIRS'. Harvard it wasn't. George's heart sank to his knees.

Still, he was there. He might as well get out and stretch his legs. The entrance to the 'museum' was tall enough for Bigfoot. On the doormat were painted two Bigfoot prints. Inside them, George's size thirteens looked small. He straightened his shoulders and entered the building.

It was even worse inside than out. The walls were papered with tattered clippings about Bigfoot sightings, all yellow with age. A maze of tables offered a jumble of Bigfoot mementoes – three or four sizes of Bigfoot statues, plastic baggies full of genuine Bigfoot hairs and toenail clippings, rubber Bigfeet ('Amaze your friends') and plaster castings of 'authentic' Bigfoot prints. A layer of dust covered them all.

George wondered what Harry would make of the 'museum'. The place gave him the creeps. He was about to leave when a voice spoke. 'I can tell by the look on your mug you think it's a load, doncha?'

Startled, George turned towards the voice. An old guy in a New York Giants baseball cap stepped into view around a moth-eaten model scene, *Bigfoot in the Wild*. He was wiping plaster off his arms.

'Well . . . ,' George said.

'Everybody asks, "Has anybody ever seen one?" Well, let me ask you: being from the city, as you obviously are, you've seen hundreds, thousands, of pigeons, right?'

George nodded yes to pigeons.

'Ever seen a baby pigeon?'

George thought about it.

'Well, neither have I,' the old guy said. 'But I got a real strong hunch they exist.' He grinned at George. 'Am I losing you yet?'

'No, not at all,' George said. 'Are you Dr Wrightwood? I'm George Henderson.'

The old guy looked George up and down, then turned to straighten some merchandise. 'Wrightwood ain't here,' he said.

'Will he be back?'

'Might be. How do you know Wrightwood?'

'His books,' George said. 'His research. He really believes in . . .' George's gesture took in all the Bigfoot paraphernalia. 'All this. I just need some answers.'

The old guy turned back to George. His voice was crusty. 'The doctor's old and tired. Spent the better part of his life chasing a dream. By the time he woke up, it was too late.'

George ripped a deposit slip out of his chequebook and wrote a note. He handed the slip to the old man. 'Well, I'd love to talk to him. My phone number's on this. If you could possibly get it to Dr Wrightwood.'

The old guy unfolded the note and read out loud: '. . . vital facts that could prevent an unnecessary and tragic end for' – he paused to laugh at George's wording – 'for the big fellow?'

George looked for a way to make himself clear. 'I have a friend, a man called, ah, Jack. And there was this giant. . .'

The old guy cocked his head. 'Is there a beanstalk involved in this, Mr Henderson?'

'A beanstalk?' For a minute George thought the old fellow had lost it. Then he realized he'd started to put Jack and giants together in the same story. 'Oh, I get it. Nope, no beanstalk. What I meant was, with all these Bigfoot sightings, what if Jack and his family opened up their home and their lives to this, ah, thing? I mean, what if it was more human than animal? And if they just said, we'll take him in. We'll accept the responsibility until there's a safe place for him to be. Not a zoo or anything like that.'

George hoped that made sense. It made perfect sense to him.

The old man looked at him quizzically. 'So, what you're saying is that you . . . excuse me, Jack, is willing to take the creature in and care for it and love it like a pet?'

George nodded. 'Like a member of the family,' he said, with conviction.

The old man shook his head. 'Noble gesture, but impossible. Sasquatch is a primitive ancestor of modern man. If you ever came face to face with one, you'd see that they are still very much animals.'

'Only on the outside,' George insisted. 'I know what I'm talking about!'

The old guy's face closed down. His voice turned gruff. 'And I know it's closing time. So if you want to talk shop, then shop.'

George shopped. At random, he picked junk off the dusty shelves until his arms were full and his wallet was empty. The old goat might not have known much about Bigfoot, but he did know about fleecing customers. George left the North American Anthropological Institute with a car full of kitsch and no answers. Once again, he had the strong and desolate feeling that he was on his own.

Doc Wrightwood watched Henderson toss his Bigfoot souvenirs into his station wagon. He felt almost guilty about not coming clean with the guy. There was something about him. Still, you couldn't be too careful. Every time there was a rash of sightings, crazies flocked to the museum like bees to a hive. Most of them wanted Sasquatch for a rug, though, not for a pet. This Henderson had a new angle.

As Henderson climbed into his car, Wrightwood could see the trouble on his face. He was pretty sure he hadn't come clean either. Something was eating him. Doc read the address on Henderson's deposit slip. Seattle. Then he folded up the paper and stuck it into the pocket of his faded flannel shirt. Just in case.

• Chapter Twenty-two

Nancy was relieved to see George pull into the driveway. She was less than delighted with the load of Bigfoot claptrap he carried into the house. There was nothing she'd consider giving her worst enemy, even for a joke. The foot lamp was, she thought, perhaps the tackiest piece of junk she'd ever seen. The way George explained it, it was the price of conversation. To Nancy it sounded like extortion.

'For a salesman, George, you've got low sales resistance.'

As soon as she said it, she was sorry. In all their years together, she'd never seen George so troubled for so long. And now his jerk of a father expected him to draw a life-size cartoon Bigfoot to help sell guns. Overnight, no less. That rated right up there with 'Why would any red-blooded male want to be an *artist*, for crying out loud?' and 'You want to marry *her*?'. Nancy disliked George's father even more than George disliked her mother. One of these days she was going to tell the old Tartar just what she thought of him.

They dumped the Bigfoot souvenirs in the living-room. George settled down at his drawing board. Nancy brought him a snack and hovered to watch him draw. The kids wandered into the room and discovered the Bigfoot junk.

'This lamp is outstanding!' Ernie cried. 'Can it go in my room?'

'You won't have to fight me for it,' Sarah told him.

'It's yours, Ernie. Take it. Please,' Nancy said. 'Don't you two have homework?'

'No,' Sarah said.

'No,' Ernie said.

Nancy sighed. No rest for the wicked. The kids had been driving her nuts ever since they got home from school that afternoon. Now they gathered around George's drawing table, while he told her about his visit to the Bigfoot Museum. The story got a little confusing in places.

'Jack and the beanstalk, George?' she asked.

'It just came out that way. I didn't know what I was saying.'

'Sounds to me like you knew exactly what you were saying,' Sarah said. 'Face it, dad. You want him back.'

George laid down his pencil and looked up at his daughter. 'Sarah, I want to *take* him back where he belongs, but that means I've got to find him first. He's an . . . an innocent. I was wrong, treating him like an animal. Maybe we somehow managed to hurt his feelings.'

'You really believe that big, dumb animal has feelings?' Sarah was incredulous.

Nancy had to smile. If Sarah hadn't been spending so much time on the telephone, she might have paid more attention to what was going on around the house.

'Yeah,' George told her. 'I believe he does. In many ways, he was one of us. Maybe even a little better, you know? Did what our kind aren't good at . . .'

'Ran around naked without getting busted,' Ernie chirped.

'I'm serious here, Ern!' George said. 'Anyhow . . .'

Sarah had taken Ernie's interruption as an opportunity to sneak away. Now that she was fifteen, she believed if an adult said more than two consecutive sentences to her, she was being lectured. Sarah hated to be lectured. George, turning back to continue his 'lecture', was surprised to find her gone.

Ernie too had reached his upper limit for serious conversation. He scooped up Little Bob and headed off for parts unknown. Peace at last. Nancy put her arms around George's neck and kissed his ear. The snarling Bigfoot on his sketch pad glared up at her. George rubbed his cheek against hers for a moment, then took up his pencil again, adding drool to the Bigfoot's pointed fangs.

Nancy rifled through the stack of sketches on the corner of the drawing board. Among the monsters she found a portrait of the smart, gentle creature they had known. She slid it out of the pile to take a better look. 'George, this is really Harry.' She looked back at the drooling villain on the sketch pad. 'Did you draw this?'

Claiming his work, George gave her a sheepish grin.

'*This* is beautiful,' Nancy said.

Modestly, George shrugged. 'It's the subject, Nan. I mean, Harry's kind of beautiful, don't you think? For a Bigfoot?'

Nancy squeezed George's shoulder. 'Prettiest one *I* ever saw,' she said.

• Chapter Twenty-three

It was night again and most creatures were inside their caves. Light shone out through the holes cut in their walls. A male creature came into view. There was a small animal with him, like the one his friends called Bob. While Harry watched, the dog squatted and left a steaming pile of droppings on the grass. The male squatted and picked up the droppings with some kind of tool. Harry was puzzled by such strange behaviour. What could it mean?

The creature and his dog went inside a cave. Harry continued his search. He moved close to a hole in the wall of another cave. A female was inside. She put leaves and roots into a large container. She put in the carcass of a small bird. Steam rose from the pot.

A sound caught Harry's attention and he turned towards its source. A male and a female creature stepped into a big bubbling pool. They had almost no hair on their bodies. Harry felt sorry for them. They must be cold.

Harry looked back to see the female in the cave pick up a small tool. She dipped it into her pot, then lifted it to her lips. When she had blown the steam away, she drank the liquid. It was food.

He looked back at the creatures in their steaming pool. Harry's stomach lurched as he understood the truth. They too were food. So the elders had been right after all.

Sounds caught his attention. They were loud and persistent but not unpleasant. He followed the sounds and peered into a house. There were many male and female creatures inside. They jumped and swayed together, in pairs, in a way that made Harry remember the mating dance of his own kind. Somehow the loud sounds seemed to match their movements.

One of the males stopped dancing. He stopped the sounds. He took one of the females by the hand and led her to a doorway. When he opened the door, an even stranger creature stood behind it. This creature was covered head to foot with thick, dark hair, yet it stood on two legs. It was the size and shape of a young Bigfoot, except its face was cruder and more animal than the faces of Harry's kind. The creature danced forward and handed something to the female. Then the male closed the door and the creature was gone.

Slowly, Harry moved around the house. The creature was outside. As Harry watched, the creature reached up, lifted off its own head and tucked it under its arm. Beneath the first, the creature had another. It was a female. The creature walked away from Harry and climbed into a car. The car drove away.

A male came out of the house. He said words to Harry. 'Hey, wait a minute.' The male moved close to Harry and held out a large green leaf. He said more words. 'Sorry. Too much excitement. Almost forgot your tip.'

Harry stared at the leaf. 'Come on,' the male said. 'Take it.' He took Harry's hand and pressed the leaf into his palm. 'You were a big hit.'

The creature went back inside. Harry ate the leaf. It was unlike any leaf he'd ever eaten, but he liked the taste.

• Chapter Twenty-four

All night, George drew. All night, his drawing style and his feelings see-sawed back and forth. They were always at odds. The tireder he got, the clearer some things became. He had spent most of his life trying to please his father. And, hard as he tried, he never quite succeeded. The old man should have had Dirty Harry for a son. That would have made him proud.

For years George had wanted his father to show some interest in his paintings. He didn't have to like them, just to acknowledge them somehow. George remembered back in fifth grade, when his father went to Open House at school and George's teacher told him his son had artistic talent. At first the old man looked embarrassed. Then he laughed. 'Thanks for the warning,' he said. 'I'll take away his colour crayons.'

Mrs Entwhistle had looked confused. 'Mr Henderson, I don't understand. Your son shows an unusual aptitude for design. He has a fine imagination. You should be very proud.'

'Proud?' the old man thundered. 'I'll be proud when he pitches a no-hitter. I'll be proud when he climbs Mount Rainier or shoots a grizzly bear. Don't ask me to be proud because he watercolours well.' He gave young George, standing beside him, a hearty slap on the back. 'And don't you worry. I'll straighten him out.'

Mrs Entwhistle started to protest. 'But Mr Henderson . . .'

George watched his father glare at his teacher. 'Whose son is he, anyway?'

'Yours, of course,' Mrs Entwhistle said.

'That's right.' His father nodded curtly. 'Don't you forget it.' With that, he whisked his son away, muttering, 'Artist, indeed.'

Nan always encouraged him to stand up to the old man.

When they were first married, she used to say, 'You want to be an artist, we'll find a way,' but first George had to prove to his father that he could provide for his family. He could just hear what the old man would have to say if Nancy went to work to help support his dreams. 'Who cares what he says, anyway?' Nan used to say. But George did. He cared deeply.

That night, sitting at his drawing board, it occurred to George that maybe he didn't care quite so much any more. The house was almost paid for. The kids were healthy and happy. He and Nan had been married for years and still loved each other. That was more than a lot of people could say. So what exactly did he have to prove?

That night, as his pencil moved across page after page, George practised not caring what his father thought. He practised saying, 'Stuff it,' inside his head. Once or twice, in the privacy of his den, he even said it out loud. Then he waited for something bad to happen. When nothing did, he smiled. 'STUFF IT,' he said, louder still.

Stuffing was fine for turkeys, of course, but Thanksgiving was still months away, and all the stuffing in the world wasn't going to produce a life-size Bigfoot by nine a.m. George studied the current version. It looked something like Walt Disney's Goofy wearing Hallowe'en vampire fangs, a bad compromise between mean and just plain silly. He crumpled it up and started again.

Around two-thirty, Nan padded in, wearing the Japanese silk kimono George had given her for their last anniversary. He liked to see her in it. 'George, come to bed.'

George pointed to his drawing. 'I've sort of got a problem, Nan. If I make him look mean and vicious, people will shoot first and then worry about the consequences. It's like drawing the "Wanted" poster of a friend. If I make him peaceful, like Harry is . . . that's not what my father's looking for.'

Nancy responded to his dilemma with an affectionate smile. 'George, I'm so happy,' she said.

'Huh?'

'I'm so proud of you,' Nancy said. 'You don't know what to do.'

At the same time he understood what Nan meant, he also

knew exactly what to do. He almost laughed out loud, it was suddenly so clear to him. His problem with the Bigfoot drawing was exactly the same as the problem with his life. Only now he had a solution.

'You go to bed,' he told Nancy. 'I'll be up in a minute.'

Now George's pencil flew across the page. He felt that his drawings hadn't come so easily or been so good since he was in the fifth grade.

Next morning George was at work early. Whistling, he spread glue on the big cardboard cut-out, then carefully unfurled his Bigfoot and laid him in place. Upright, he looked terrific. George waltzed him into the hunting department and put him in place in the display window, next to the sighting map.

There. George was pleased. His Bigfoot looked just like Harry. When it came right down to it, making the fur look three-dimensional had been the hardest part. He'd even managed that funny kind of half-smile Harry had. George poured himself a cup of coffee from the Bunn Automatic and joked around with the guys until his dad showed up.

There was no mistaking it when he did. 'GEORGE!' the old man roared.

'Yes, dad?'

'Front and centre. Forward march. NOW.' When his father used military jargon, it meant that he was really mad. George's fellow employees shot him sympathetic looks as his father marched him towards the front of the store. George smiled benignly back at them.

'Outside!' the old man ordered.

George held the door open for him. 'I take it you've already seen my drawing. What do you think?'

The old man exploded. 'I wanted King Kong and you bring me a goddamned giant gerbil. I told you exactly what to do, and you didn't even come close.'

George felt his stomach start to knot up the way it always had when his father yelled at him. Lucky he'd rehearsed his response. He said it without the slightest stammer. 'Well, maybe it's right on the nose. What if he's not vicious? What if he's some kind of man? Maybe he's gentle . . . has feelings . . .'

George didn't get to finish his speech. 'Where did you dream up that garbage? Go stick a pin on Queen Anne Hill. We've just had another sighting.'

George moved off to do his father's bidding. It beat a fight. Behind him he heard his father mumble, 'I shoulda got a real artist.'

George shook his head. There was no winning with the old man.

From inside the window, George's Bigfoot flashed his friendly smile at George's father. The old man growled.

• Chapter Twenty-five

LaFleur cruised through streets lined with middle-class split-level houses until the congregation of news vans, police cars and spectators told him he'd found the right place. He parked the power wagon, climbed out and hurried into the crowd. These tracks would be fresh if the clods hadn't trampled them already. His eyes scanned for prints on the well-kept lawn.

'Morning, Jocko.' A familiar voice spoke near his ear. LaFleur looked up to see Doc Wrightwood. It was the last place he would have expected to meet him. In the woods, maybe. 'What are you doing here, Wally?'

Hands in his pockets, Doc shrugged. 'Curiosity. Trying to figure out why anybody would go to such extremes to fake these ridiculous sightings. I'm not surprised to find you here.'

Jacques hated the old man's riddles. 'What the hell's that supposed to mean?' he asked.

Doc gave him one of his cynical smiles. 'You're not trying to raise money for a new expedition, are you, Jocko?'

No one could make Jacques angrier. 'Listen, old man. You believe what you want. But he's real and he's here. I don't know why or how. But he's here. Out of his element, and very vulnerable.'

Doc grinned at him. 'You're scratchin' at straws, Jock. Give it up, why don't you? Life's too short.'

'Jacques LaFleur does not give up. In a short while, I'll have your "baby pigeon". I'll stake my reputation on it.'

Wrightwood took his hands out of his pockets. In his right he held a crumpled bill. 'I'll do better than that, Jock. I'll bet you five bucks.' Laughing, he waved the five under LaFleur's nose.

LaFleur was too angry to speak. He sputtered instead. He'd make the old cretin eat his five. Jacques comforted himself with thoughts of the glory to come.

• Chapter Twenty-six

The night before Christmas had never seen the store so crowded. Everyone – young, old, housewives and businessmen, city slickers and sportsmen – all knew exactly what they wanted. They wanted guns.

Every salesman in the place was working the hunting-department, and still the queues were six deep. George found it hard to sell and worry at the same time. Every gun he sold might be the one that nailed his friend. George dawdled. He developed a speech impediment. He parted with the merchandise reluctantly. Around him, his fellow employees passed out weapons as efficiently and unfeelingly as if they were bricks of government cheese.

Between customers, Stuart elbowed George. 'What's the matter, Henderson? You sick or something?'

'Now that you mention it, I do feel sort of funny,' George said.

A would-be marksman collared Stuart. Someone tugged at George's sleeve. He looked down into the wild eyes of a tiny blue-haired lady. 'What kind of gun do I need to protect myself against a Bigfoot?' she demanded.

The old girl should have been home knitting booties for the great-grandkids. George didn't want to take her money any more than he wanted to give her a weapon. He leaned down and spoke in a low voice. 'Believe me, you don't need protection. They're harmless. They eat sugar cubes.'

Just then a very wild-eyed, very excited man came panting up. He pushed the old lady aside. 'I need a gun. I need a big, big gun. Maybe one of those Dirty Harry Magnums. Or an M-16. Will those go fully automatic?'

'Full autos are illegal,' George took pleasure in informing

him, 'and handguns take seven days to clear. I'm afraid if you want a gun right now, it will have to be a rifle or a shotgun.'

'Give me the biggest one you've got. Anything with a night 'scope?'

George was wondering how he could look himself in the mirror the next morning if he actually sold a gun to this bozo. He stalled. 'Well, we've got some big guns, and we've got some big, big guns, but I think we're out of big, big ammo.'

The customer stared at George as if he'd lost his marbles. So, George noticed, did Stuart and Billers.

'Look, pal.' The customer leaned across the counter to speak confidentially to George. 'They've just spotted that thing not three blocks from my house. I've got a family to protect. I need a gun NOW!'

'Where do you live?' George pulled out his receipt book to make the question seem more reasonable. 'It's for the gun. Just a few questions.'

'One-one-four-eight-four Devon Drive,' the man told George.

Quickly George wrote the address down. 'And where was the sighting?'

'At the corner of Maple and Overview. Hey, what's that got to do with it?'

George tossed the receipt book on to the counter and headed for the door. He knew where he belonged. It wasn't here. He was on his way out the door when he ran smack into the old man, who was manoeuvring the eight-foot Bigfoot cut-out. 'See?' his dad said. 'You're not the only artist in the family.'

George saw. The old man had taken a magic marker to George's masterpiece. He had drawn points on Harry's teeth. He had made his eyebrows frown. He had done it badly. What's more, he was proud of himself.

'Not bad for an arthritic old shooter, huh?'

For the first time in his life, George yelled at his old man. 'What have you done? The way I did it was right. You shouldn't have changed it.'

His dad looked stunned. He backpedalled. 'Okay, George, cool down. It's just a piece of cardboard.'

'Not to me,' George informed his father. 'It means something to me. *He* means something to me.'

As George spoke, the old man's expression changed from blank to bewildered. 'What the hell are you talking about?'

George showed him before he told him. He ripped the assistant manager badge off his sportcoat and stuffed it in his father's pocket. To make sure the old man got the message, he said, 'I quit!'

Marching out of the store, George felt ten years younger and ten pounds lighter. Amazing how much that badge had weighed.

His father called after him. 'Over this? You can't quit. We've never been so busy. What the hell's the matter with you?' The farther away George got, the louder his father yelled. 'WHY ARE YOU DOING THIS?'

A smile just tickled the corners of George's lips. He didn't turn back. Old man Ronan called after him, but that didn't stop George. If he didn't have a job tomorrow – well, he'd worry about that tomorrow. Right now he had more important things on his mind.

As he started the station wagon, George pulled his city map out of the glove compartment, got it folded the right way and looked for Overview. He didn't know the south part of the city too well. The freeway entrance he needed was closed for repairs, and the detour to the next one snarled him up in downtown traffic. A real scenic tour. Finally, he was on his way.

Around the intersection of Maple and Overview, it looked like a carnival or – George remembered the police sergeant's words – a war zone. Cops, reporters, paramedics everywhere. George elbowed his way through a tangle of onlookers and found a couple of firemen plastering a bandage on a small bald man in an expensive jogging suit. Beside him a cop crouched down, notebook in hand. George approached the policeman.

'Excuse me. How long ago did this happen?'

The policeman shot him an exasperated look. 'Do you mind? I'm taking a statement here.'

George backed off and looked around. A badly mangled bicycle lay in the street. George deduced that it belonged to the guy with the bandages. The guy was waving his hands as he talked to the cop. George tuned in.

'. . . huge, gigantic. A monster. A rabid ape, but bigger than a regular rabid ape. I mean, uh . . .'

Beside the witness, the policeman gritted his teeth. 'Just calm down and tell me exactly what happened.'

'Okay. I'm okay. I brought my poor ten-speed Roadmaster to a complete stop, like I always do at stop signs . . .'

'It's okay, fella,' the policeman said. 'I'm not here to pass out tickets.'

By now a gaggle of reporters, TV and press, had found the action. A bouquet of microphones blossomed around cop and witness. All the attention went to the little guy's head. George figured he wanted to make the five o'clock news.

'. . . when out of nowhere, this humongous hairy thing is standing right in front of me, growling with these enormous fangs, and giant hands . . . and he grabs me and, uh, he picks me up, bike and all, over his head, and then he smashes me down on the cement.' It didn't sound like Harry to George. He got the feeling the guy was making all this up as he went along.

'And now he's all over me, snarling, his pointed teeth dripping with saliva, so I . . . I grab my mace and . . .'

That's when George lost it. The thought of this little lying creep macing Harry was more than George could stand. 'You what? Mace! You idiot!'

The little creep cringed as George advanced. The policeman stepped between them. 'Hold on. Stay back.'

The creep spoke to the cop. 'I didn't really mace him. But, but I was about to be eaten.'

'Eaten?' George roared. 'By a vegetarian? You, you . . .' George took a deep breath. 'I don't doubt that you saw him, but what *really* happened is that when you saw him, you were so scared, out of your mind, that you crashed your, your dumb Roadmaster into the stop sign, bumped your head on the kerb here and probably scared him half to death in the process.'

The policeman started to ask a question, but George wasn't through. 'I'm right, aren't I? That's what *really* happened, isn't it?'

The little creep cracked. 'Yes. Yes, that's what happened.'

There. Harry was cleared. George had never heard such a ridiculous story in his life. No wonder things got out of hand, with people running around making up tales like that. For a moment, George felt like Captain America. Suddenly, the press were thrusting their microphones in *his* face. The questions came thick and fast.

'How did you know this?'

'Did you see it happen?'

'What's your name, sir?'

'My name is George Hen . . .' George came to his senses in time to swallow the last two syllables of his name. Harry was out there somewhere, in danger. Harry needed him a whole lot more than George needed publicity. He waved the microphones aside. 'Uh, I have to leave now. Sorry. Goodbye.'

'But Mr Hen! Mr Hen! Just a few quick questions, sir,' the press called after him.

George hurried back to the station wagon. The most intrepid of the reporters dogged him all the way, but George Hen didn't say another word.

• Chapter Twenty-seven

Nancy kept the TV on all morning, listening for Bigfoot news. She wasn't disappointed. There was a major sighting. A man on a bicycle claimed to have been accosted by a monster.

'And now a report from Phil Cheever and our mobile news unit at the scene . . .'

There was a brief knock at the back door. Irene let herself in. 'Morning, Nan. Everything okay here?'

Finger to her lips, Nancy nodded. 'Shhh. I'm watching the news. Bigfoot.'

'Ah, that's all a lot of hooey.' Irene helped herself to coffee in her favourite mug.

'Let's see if we can't pick this up,' Phil Cheever said. His microphone joined half a dozen others in front of a bald man patched with bandages.

Irene sat down at the kitchen table. 'What happened to him?'

'. . . and, uh, he picks me up, bike and all, over his head, and then he smashes me down on the cement. And now he's all over me, snarling . . .'

'Bigfoot?' Irene said. 'That sounds more like Jack the Ripper.'

'. . . so I grab my mace and . . .'

'That's a good idea,' Irene said. 'Maybe I ought to carry a mace.'

Nancy heard a familiar voice. She turned around, expecting to see George in the doorway. George wasn't there.

'Eaten! By a vegetarian? You, you . . .' George's voice.

Irene craned forward towards the screen. 'Say, isn't that . . . ?'

Nancy switched off the set.

'That guy sure looked like George. Sounded like him too,' Irene said.

'Don't be silly,' Nancy told her neighbour. 'It couldn't be George. George is at work.'

'Must be his double then,' Irene said. 'People have them, you know. I read this article in the *Star* . . .'

'Tell me all about it,' Nancy said.

Break. Ernie popped a leaf in his mouth and pretended to chew. 'Oh boy, is this ever good,' he growled.

Frankie MacDowell lowered the baseball-bat rifle he'd been pointing at Ernie's heart. 'Come on, Ernie. If you can't do it right, let somebody else be Bigfoot.'

'Oh, I suppose you know everything about Bigfoot,' Ernie said.

'I know he's big and mean and wild. He doesn't go around munching leaves, for cripe's sake,' Frankie said.

'Oh yeah?'

'Yeah.'

'Well, watch this,' Ernie said. He filled his lungs and let out his biggest, best imitation of Harry's roar. Then he knocked the baseball bat out of Frankie's hands and ran like crazy.

'Get him, men,' Frankie hollered. 'Get the Bigfoot!'

The chase was on.

Bigfoot. Bigfoot. That's all anybody could talk about. Sarah was sick of it. She'd had enough Bigfoot to last a lifetime. In biology, fourth period, someone asked the teacher, Mr Krebs, if there was such a thing.

'There is absolutely no scientific evidence to suggest that Bigfoot exists,' Krebs told the class.

'Then what's everybody so excited about?' someone in the third row asked.

'Well,' Mr Krebs said, 'if there were such a thing as Bigfoot, and if somebody caught one, it could be scientifically very important. Those are several big ifs. But *if* all those ifs were true, we would probably have found the missing link between animal and man.'

Sarah's new lab partner, Jamie Conway, leaned over the

dissecting pan and whispered, 'What do you think of all this Bigfoot business, anyway?'

'Personally, I think it's highly overrated,' Sarah whispered back.

'May I be excused now?' Sarah asked when she finished her supper.

She was already out of her chair when George said, 'No. Sit down, honey. I have an important announcement to make.'

'You've found Harry!' Ernie guessed.

Nancy held her breath.

'No, Ern. I haven't found him,' George said. 'But I havc quit my job.'

For a moment Nancy was too surprised to say a thing. The whole family greeted the news with silence.

George looked at each of them in turn. 'Well?'

Nancy spoke first. 'George, that's wonderful!'

Sarah looked at her in disbelief. 'What's so wonderful about it?'

'Was Grandpa mad?' Ernie asked.

George grinned. 'Very.'

Nancy clapped her hands in delight. 'Oh, George. I wish I could have seen his face.'

'Yeah,' George said. 'The old man was pretty upset.'

'How did it happen?' Nancy asked. 'What drove you to it? I want to know everything.'

'Well,' George said, 'it's kind of a long story. But when I saw what he'd done to my Bigfoot, I just saw red. Yelled at him. I think I told him off pretty good.'

'I suppose this means I won't be getting my allowance on Saturday,' Sarah said. 'I suppose this means I'll have to go back to work at Burger King.'

Nancy shot her a calming look. 'We're not sure what it means yet, honey. Give us time to think it through.'

'You know what I think?' Sarah said. 'I think you think more of that smelly Bigfoot than you do of your own family.'

'Harry. Right,' George said. 'That's the other thing. I have to find Harry.'

Ernie jumped up from his chair. 'What are we waiting for? I'll go with you, dad. Sarah, you go with mom.'

'Calm down, son,' George said. 'Nobody's going anywhere. It's not safe out there. I know. I spent half the day arming idiots. This is something I'd better try alone.'

'Great!' Sarah said. 'First he tells us we're going to be poor. Now he says I'm going to be an orphan.'

'Sarah, don't over-dramatize,' Nancy said, in her most no-nonsense voice. She looked to George. He looked . . . different. Good. Nancy thought she'd never loved him so much. 'Do you have a plan, George?'

'Yep,' George said. 'I have. I'm going to stop by the store first, and then I'm going to hit the streets.'

'How come you're going to the store, dad?' Ernie asked. 'I thought you quit.'

George smiled at Ernie. 'Let's put it this way, son. If you think Grandpa's mad tonight, just wait until tomorrow.'

'Wow,' Ernie said.

'Please be careful, George,' Nancy said.

'I will,' George promised. 'Don't worry about me.'

• Chapter Twenty-eight

George left home after dark. The city rose up eerily between the freeway and the bay, its nocturnal glow made hazy by a light fog. The full moon topped the tallest of the city's towers, shrinking and paling as it rose. George had lived in Seattle all his life. Just an hour before, he would have said he knew it like the back of his hand. Now he was struck by its size, by its complexity, by how much he did not know. Tonight, as he took his accustomed freeway exit and followed familiar streets to the store where he had worked for more than twenty years, he noticed things that he had never seen before.

He imagined he was Harry, trying to find his way safely through the urban maze. Suddenly George felt lost in his home town.

At the store George punched in the code to disarm the security system and let himself in the back way. The tall shelves of the stockroom were spooky in the darkness, and huge shipping cartons, not yet unpacked, loomed like monsters. Since he had quit, George felt like an intruder.

He went out to the front and confronted the giant stuffed grizzly with its stiff-jawed snarl. 'Well, buddy,' he said. 'It's you and me. Take it easy, now, big boy. This won't hurt a bit.' George took out the big rasp he'd brought from home and set to work. The job wasn't as hard as he'd imagined it might be. With a good manicure and his fangs filed flat, Claws didn't look so ferocious any more. In fact, he almost seemed to be smiling.

George studied his handiwork. A new thought struck him, and he laughed out loud. It was really the old man he wanted to de-fang. Like father, like bear. With his teeth blunted, the old man's bark was probably a whole lot worse than his bite. It was just that George had never dared put it to the test before. He considered the possibility that if he stood up straight and looked the old curmudgeon in the eye, he might actually come to *like* his dad. He considered the possibility that his dad might like him better if he did. It was a long shot, but George was willing to give it a try.

He scribbled a note on the back of a store receipt and pinned it to the grizzly's chest. It said simply, 'Dad, I love you. G.' How could anybody argue with that?

That done, George climbed into the display window for a last look at the Bigfoot sighting map. The pattern of the pushpins seemed to confirm his hunch. Harry was downtown tonight.

George reset the alarm system, locked up the store and hit the streets.

• Chapter Twenty-nine

Harry moved cautiously inside the forest of tall caves. Here his feet left no prints on the hard pathways. All the smells of this place were strange to him, all of its sounds. Here and there, small trees and shrubs grew in little containers full of earth, and Harry helped himself to what leaves he could pick in passing. Still, his stomach felt empty. He did not know if he would ever find his home.

He moved close to the fronts of buildings, trying to stay out of the light. The holes in the buildings were filled with something clear and hard and shiny. Sometimes he saw himself reflected in it. At first he thought it was another Bigfoot, not himself, but when he reached out to touch the other, all he could feel was the coldness of the glass. Slowly he came to realize it was himself he saw. Harry moved on.

He came to a lighted window with many picture boxes arrayed inside it. They were like the picture box in the home of his friend. He had watched it with the young male. Now, as he looked at the boxes, the face of his friend, the male creature, appeared on them. Harry roared greetings. On the faces of the different boxes there were many pictures of his friend. A metal fence separated Harry from the boxes. Until he removed it, his friend would not be able to see or hear him. He shook the metal fence until it gave way. When it did, a loud bell began to shrill. Harry did not like the sound of it. He smashed through the clear shiny stuff and reached out for the box with the picture of the male. Harry lifted the box to his lips and licked his friend's face. Harry knew it was not skin he touched, but he was happy. He would take the box with him on his journey.

The box was on some kind of leash. When Harry stepped away from the building, the surface of the picture box grew dark. His friend disappeared. Harry threw the picture box away and went to get another. The same thing happened again. As he moved away, the box went dark. His friend died. When he looked back to the lighted boxes, his friend was gone.

A car came screaming around the corner and fixed its lights on him. Harry sensed he was in danger. He lifted the picture box high above his head and flung it at the approaching car. The box exploded in the street. The car swerved and smashed into the face of a building across the street. Creatures, all males, jumped from the car and pointed guns at him.

Harry made for the safety of a nearby alley.

• Chapter Thirty

For a while George cruised. Uptown, around the posh department stores and slick boutiques, the streets were all but empty. Heading west, he peered into the shadows of the Pike Place Market, closed for the night. South, towards Pioneer Square, there was more night life. Strains of jukebox music wafted out of open tavern doors. Drunks staggered up the street or took rest in the doorways of the older office buildings where lawyers plied their trade by day. On top of the dark courthouse he could see the lighted windows of the county jail.

George decided to concentrate his search between First and Third, south of Pike Street and north of King. It was a long stretch of three main avenues, stitched together by a maze of alleys. There were lots of recessed doorways, places to hide. A wary creature could easily stay out of sight.

When George reached the area, a swelling crowd of freelance Rambos and city police confirmed his intuition. The blue lights of police cars tore the sky. Sirens rose around him. As George was about to turn on to First, a police car squealed into his path. When it stopped, officers climbed out and sealed the street. George backed up and drove away from the excitement. On a street that seemed safely deserted, George nosed the station wagon into a hillside parking place and set out on foot. He looked around. There was no one to see him slip into the alley.

With his trigger finger Jacques traced the thick black line that connected sightings on his map. Bigfoot was in downtown Seattle. Now. Tonight. If Jacques LaFleur could help it, the Sasquatch would never leave. A lifetime of tracking and a box of cartridges said so. In the darkness of his power wagon LaFleur threw back his head and laughed out loud.

He headed down Pine Street towards what his calculations told him was prime hunting ground. As he prepared to turn left on Third, a policeman flagged him down. A small battalion of gendarmes was setting up barricades. LaFleur rolled down his window.

'Area's closed, buddy,' the officer said. 'Third to First, from here down past the Kingdome. No civilians allowed in the area.'

'Why's that? You chasing terrorists? Bank robbers, maybe?'

'We have reason to believe that Bigfoot is in the area.'

'What reason?' LaFleur asked.

But the cop said, 'Look, fella. I've got work to do here. Now move along. You'll have to find yourself a detour. Try going north a few blocks, then cut down to Alaskan.'

For a moment LaFleur considered offering his services to the police. 'Excuse me, officer, but I am a seasoned hunter. I have been tracking Bigfoot for years.' He thought better of it. If he helped the police find Bigfoot, they would take credit for it. They would keep the hide. No, he was going to have to outwit the police.

LaFleur nodded to the officer and backed into Pine Street, then turned right in case the cop was paying attention. Out of their sight, he circled back to the mid-point of the cordoned area and parked his wagon. Rifle under his arm, he slipped past the barricades. What was meant to keep him out would also contain his prey. How nice of the police to isolate the area for him. Now all he had to do was beat them to Bigfoot.

Noise spilled into the alley from the intersection. From the sound of it, there was quite a crowd out there. Flattened against the side of a building, George crept towards the alley's mouth and peered out at the scene. A cop car, its top light spinning, blocked the street. Uniformed officers surrounded the car and held back the growing crowd, while the boss cop studied a city map spread on the bonnet.

The boss cop looked up and barked at his men. 'I want this quadrant airtight. Nothing gets out. Nothing! And no force, except in self-defence. I don't need some prankster in a monkey suit bleeding all over the streets. Now move!'

The clump of officers dispersed in all directions. Swinging their nightsticks, a pair made for George's alley. He inched deeper into shadow and held his breath as they passed him.

Jacques moved soundlessly through the city alleys. He could hear distant voices, but here it was quiet. He rounded a corner and was almost startled by the bulk of a dump truck parked in the alley. A large scoop was mounted on the front of the truck, and its engine was running, but its drivers were gone. LaFleur resumed his tracking. It was a hard job on cement, but when he looked down, he was rewarded. In a half-dried puddle he found what he was looking for – a perfect Bigfoot imprint in the mud. Its toes pointed towards the garbage truck. LaFleur followed.

Deer hunting had never been like this. George's heart pounded. Despite the autumn chill, he was sweating freely. The road showed no trail. And George felt hunted. He'd never been in competition with the cops before. His progress was slow. Too slow. He wished there were a way to cover more ground faster.

There was. It was risky, but his voice could go farther and faster than his legs could. He slipped around a corner, determined to try. A low rumble startled him, until he realized it was only the sound of an engine idling. George took a few deep breaths, then whispered Harry's name a few times before he realized that Harry didn't know that it was his name.

George rose up to his full height and filled his lungs with air. Then he threw back his head and let loose his best imitation of Harry's thunderous howl. His voice grew even bigger as it bounced off walls.

Only twice before in all his years of tracking Sasquatch had Jacques heard the huge, full-bodied howl that echoed through the alley now, but there was no mistaking it. His quarry was nearby. Jacques hid himself in the darkness of a doorway and looked out, his hunter's senses on full alert. A huge shadow loomed against the wall opposite his hiding place. LaFleur took off the safety and readied his rifle for action.

George walked slowly and deliberately, defying the light that shone behind him. He almost felt like Sasquatch when he summoned up another ear-splitting howl. George stopped and waited for an answer from his friend.

When Sasquatch howled again, adrenalin surged through LaFleur's body, sharpening his every reflex. He shouldered his rifle and moved towards the intersection. A third call thundered, filling the alley with its echoes. Jacques whipped around, his weapon ready. A shadow twice as big as the first one loomed against the wall. He turned back to the smaller shadow. It was running now. Jacques turned again to the place where the shadows should intersect.

A dark, hairy mass filled his vision, just as a strong musk stench filled his nostrils. After more than thirty years of searching, Jacques found himself just inches from his prey. The sheer animal mass of Bigfoot numbed him. His only reflex, for the moment, was awe.

The Bigfoot seized Jacques's rifle. Jacques let go. The rifle fell. When it hit the ground, it fired. The explosion annoyed the creature. His massive hands closed on Jacques and lifted him high in the air. In a long arc, LaFleur flew through the night. He landed painfully. Then everything went dark.

At the sound of a nearby rifle shot, George nearly jumped out of his skin. When his brain kicked in again, it was full of fear for Harry. It sounded as if the cops, or one of the crazies, had found him first. Well, maybe there was still something George could do for his friend. He advanced slowly. With apprehension, he rounded the corner.

HARRY. Unharmed. Unscathed. George's heart expanded in his chest. Breathing thanks, he raced towards the Bigfoot, arms wide, and found himself enfolded in a powerful embrace.

The sound of running footsteps dispersed their joy. George could hear the clatter of hardware that he did not doubt was weapons. Even as they listened, the sounds drew nearer. A metallic clunk rang from the dump truck. Harry responded with a low growl.

George turned towards the idling truck. 'Get in!' he told Harry. 'Come on, hop in. They'll never look for you up here!'

George headed for the cab, expecting Harry to climb in beside him. There was a small failure in communication. Harry climbed into the scoop instead. At least he was out of sight. In the wing mirror George saw the shadows of running men. He ground the truck into gear and started down the alley. Behind them the intersection filled up with cops.

In the scoop the smell was terrible. Worse yet, there was a creature there, the male Harry had disarmed and thrown aside before. Instinctively, Harry knew the creature meant him harm. As he watched, the male's eyes opened. Harry growled at him. He stared at Harry, then reached behind him and drew a small gun from his coat.

All of a sudden, the truck lurched to a stop. Harry and the male slammed against the metal side of the scoop. The creature dropped his gun. Harry picked it up and looked at it. The truck moved forward. Harry could feel the creature's fear.

The police were hot on his tail. George examined the dashboard of the garbage truck. He slammed on the brake and released one of the levers. The back end of the truck dropped off, spewing garbage, but the scoop held fast in front. It would take the cops a while to dig themselves out. George threw the truck into gear again and stamped on the accelerator.

When the truck stopped for a second time, the Bigfoot dropped Jacques's pistol. It planted itself, butt up, in a mess of rotting melons. Without taking his eyes from the creature, LaFleur crawled forwards and reached for his gun. There. He had it. He cleared the soft, stinking mess from the barrel and aimed the pistol.

With the police slowed down behind, it looked as if they were free. Thirty yards and they'd be out of the alley, back on city streets. With any luck, they'd be in the station wagon and on their way home before the cops knew what had hit them. George kept the accelerator flat to the floorboards.

Suddenly a man staggered into the alley. The headlights illuminated him as the truck zoomed forward. He was dressed in tatters, red-faced and very drunk. A wino. And George was about to blow the guy to kingdom come.

This was it, the moment he'd waited almost a lifetime for. His pistol was in his hand, his finger curled around the trigger. He aimed at the creature's heart. Whenever he imagined killing Sasquatch, it was in the woods, but LaFleur was not about to argue with fate. A garbage scoop would have to do. His finger teased the trigger.

George hit the brakes. The wino squatted in front of the garbage truck and shielded his head with crossed arms.

Jacques cocked the hammer back. Slowly, steadily, his trigger finger squeezed.

The brakes grabbed just in time. The truck shuddered to a stop so violently that the scoop flew off the front. It sailed through the air, hit the ground and skidded, shooting sparks.

Before he could fire the truck lurched, and a slimy, stinking wall of garbage crashed down on Jacques. Damp coffee grounds rained into his eyes. The scoop was airborne. With a bone-rattling crash, it landed and skidded, flattening LaFleur against a mound of soggy trash. Dripping slime, Bigfoot rose above him. LaFleur had never imagined the creature would kill *him*. He closed his eyes and waited to die.

Blinking and looking dazed, Harry peered out of the scoop.

'We did it!' George hollered. 'Come on, boy!'

Harry climbed out. His fur was covered with garbage. Even from a distance, he reeked. George didn't care. The station wagon was right around the corner. He grabbed Harry's hand and tugged him towards it. They both climbed in. As George started the engine, Harry modified the design. He sat up straight and made himself another dome in the roof. They sped away.

• Chapter Thirty-one

Jacques waited, but nothing happened. Cautiously he opened one eye, in time to see the monster clambering out of the scoop. Jacques rose up on one elbow and wiped his face with his shirtsleeve. His body ached all over, but nothing seemed to be broken. Bigfoot had let him live. His mistake.

LaFleur rose to his knees, then to his feet, and struggled to the side of the scoop. He arrived in time to see a very peculiar station wagon, with two large welts rising from its metal roof, drive past the intersection before him. Sasquatch sat in the passenger seat. Jacques just had time to read the rear number plate before the station wagon disappeared. It matched the number on the plate he'd found beside the highway. George Henderson was Bigfoot's chauffeur.

Footsteps sounded in the alley, growing louder. LaFleur dug in the garbage to retrieve his pistol. Just as he grabbed the handle, he lost his footing on an over-ripe avocado and fell hard into the garbage. He scrambled to his feet, pistol ready, and peered over the side of the scoop. A forest of guns blossomed around his head.

'Hold it right there, fella,' a policeman ordered.

Jacques froze.

The police took his pistol. They handcuffed him. They laughed at the way he looked and smelled. Then the officer in charge, Sergeant Schwarz, held up his rifle, lost in the alley. 'Ever see this before? It's got your initials on it, just like this pistol here.'

Jacques said nothing. The officer flashed him a wicked grin. 'Well, well. I'm sure you have a concealed weapon permit. I'd like to see it.'

'You can't do this,' Jacques said. 'A man's got a right to protect himself. I want to talk to my lawyer.'

Schwarz laughed. 'Yeah, sure. Maybe you and your pals can chip in for one. Save yourself some dough.' He turned to an underling. 'Okay, take him away.'

The officer swung open the door of a large police van. It was already full of handcuffed men. Some wore hunting jackets. The rest were dressed from movies – *Road Warrior*, *Rambo*. There was even a cowboy hat or two. 'Welcome to the Bigfoot Brigade,' the cop said. He prodded Jacques from behind with his nightstick. 'Come on. Climb in there with your buddies.'

Jacques turned to Sergeant Schwarz. 'Wait. You're making a big mistake. Do you know who I am? I am Jacques LaFleur, the world's foremost Bigfoot hunter. Surely you recognize my name. I can help you.'

'You can help me by climbing into the van, Mr La Flour.'

'I know where Bigfoot is,' Jacques told them. 'I can take you to him.'

'Sure,' Schwarz said with a grin.

'This is no laughing matter,' Jacques said.

'Who's laughing?' Schwarz said. 'Bunch of crazies like you guys almost makes you want to vote for gun control.'

'You . . . you communist!' Jacques shouted, as the van doors slammed shut behind him. 'You won't get by with this.'

• Chapter Thirty-two

Ernie hovered around the kitchen television. He used to hate it when they interrupted his favourite shows with news – news bulletins were *boring* – but tonight he wanted more updates and fewer laughs. How was he supposed to care about the dumb problems of some fake family when his own dad was out there in the mean streets and the cops were after Harry?

'Is your homework done?' his mom asked.

'How can I concentrate on spelling words at a time like this?'

'Get your book,' his mother said. 'I'll test you.'

'Mom . . .'

'Get it.'

Ernie got his spelling book. They settled at the kitchen table and his mom turned the TV volume down. 'We'll keep the picture on,' she promised. 'We can turn the sound up if something happens.' She opened the book. 'Lesson One. Spell "danger".'

Ernie thought about it. 'D-A-I-N-J-E-R.'

'Wrong,' his mom said. 'Try again.'

'Look, mom.' Ernie pointed to the TV screen. The news announcer was talking. His mother turned the volume up just as the picture switched to the mobile news van downtown.

The TV reporter was standing in front of a police barricade in his trenchcoat. 'In response to Bigfoot sightings in downtown Seattle, police have closed streets to civilian traffic. Earlier this evening a Third Avenue television and stereo store was broken into and vandalized. Police now believe that the culprit was . . .' – the announcer couldn't help smiling – 'get this: Bigfoot! We'll keep you posted on events as they develop. Meanwhile, back to you, Dave.'

Dave appeared at his news desk. 'Thanks, Phil. I wonder what Bigfoot wants with a stereo? Well, more later. Now back to our regularly scheduled programming.'

His mother turned the sound off. 'So far, so good,' she said.

'What's good about it?' Ernie asked.

'They haven't shot Harry and they haven't arrested your father,' Mom said. 'That's good. Spell "friend".'

'Jeez, mom, give me a break.'

'Spell it.'

'H-A-R-R-Y,' Ernie said. For a minute he thought his mother was going to get mad, but then she smiled at him.

Sarah came in and browsed in the refrigerator. 'There's nothing to eat,' she complained.

'Are you finally off the phone?' Mom asked.

'For now,' Sarah said. 'I promised I'd call Sasha back after I read the English assignment.'

'What are you reading?' Mom asked.

'*The Call of the Wild*,' Sarah said. 'It's boring.'

'Sarah, I want you to stay off the phone for the rest of the night,' Mom said. 'Your father might need to reach us.'

'Mom,' Sarah said, 'I promised Sasha. Anyway, I don't see what's the big deal.'

'Well, I don't want your father waiting,' Mom said. 'You can explain to Sasha in the morning.'

'Yo, mom,' Ernie said. He turned to Sarah. 'You gotta zip your lip, motor mouth.'

'Zip your face,' Sarah said. 'Besides, if you're not nice to me, I won't tell you the Bigfoot joke Sasha told me.'

'A Bigfoot joke,' Ernie said. 'Wow.'

'Go on,' Mom said. 'The suspense is killing me.'

'Well, okay. What do you call one-tenth of a Bigfoot?'

Ernie loved riddles. He thought about it. 'How about "sir"?'

'Wrong,' Sarah said. 'Mom?'

Mom shook her head. 'I have no idea.'

Sarah grinned, delivering the punch line. 'A big toe. Get it?'

Mom groaned. Ernie said, 'That's dumb.'

'It's better than your stupid jokes, Ernie. Like "Why did the chicken cross the road? To get a peanut butter and jelly sandwich."'

'That's a very funny joke,' Ernie said. 'You just don't have any sense of humour.'

'Kids,' Mom said. It was her cool-it voice.

'Well, back to the books,' Sarah said. She grabbed a bag of potato chips from the cupboard and headed upstairs.

Ernie turned to his mother. 'Mom, do you think dad's all right?'

'I hope so, Ernie,' Mom said. 'I'm believing both he and Harry are just fine until we hear otherwise. You know what they say – no news is good news.'

Ernie thought about that. 'What's that supposed to mean?'

'I'm not quite sure,' his mother said.

At nine o'clock Nancy told Ernie to go to bed. He didn't want to go.

At nine thirty she told Ernie to go to bed. 'Please, mom, just let me stay up a little longer.'

At ten o'clock, Nancy said, 'Come on, Ern. Come sit with me. We'll wait for dad together.' By ten fifteen Ernie was sound asleep beside her on the sofa. Gently she took off his glasses and put them on the coffee table. He was a good kid, especially when asleep. Nancy stroked Ernie's hair back off his forehead and tried to imagine what was happening to George.

At ten thirty the phone rang. Nancy answered before it woke Ernie. 'Are you all right? Where are you?'

'I'm in the kitchen,' Irene said, 'and I'm fine, except we're all out of prune juice. I wondered if you guys had some.'

'Not a prune in the house,' Nancy said.

'I was just wondering,' Irene said. 'Well, I guess I'll go to bed now.'

'Good idea,' Nancy said. 'Goodnight, Irene.'

At eleven o'clock Nancy watched the news. The only new information was that police were arresting all the armed maniacs who'd run downtown to shoot Bigfoot. The ones they showed all looked like criminals and crazies. George didn't have a gun. Nancy wasn't sure if that was good or bad. She started to doze off, wondering.

The telephone woke her up. 'Is Betty there?'

'No Betty here. Wrong number.'

At midnight Nancy dozed off.

Around one in the morning, something woke them. It was the living-room light. Slowly Nancy opened her eyes. George was home. He was safe.

'Harry!' Ernie exclaimed.

'George. Where the hell have you been?' Nancy said. 'We've been worried.' She saw the Sasquatch beside her husband. 'Harry. Welcome home.'

Sarah came trotting down the stairs. 'I knew it was him.' She turned to Harry. 'I could smell you all the way upstairs.'

'Rrrrfff.' Little Bob raced down the stairs, skidding on the hardwood floors, and sprang up on the back of the couch. He took a flying leap. Harry palmed him like a basketball.

'Looks like it's unanimous,' George said.

Nancy bounced up off the sofa. 'Let's celebrate.'

Sarah groaned. 'Let's move.'

George held up his hand to catch the family's attention. When everyone was quiet, he turned to Harry. 'You may not understand a word of this, Harry, but I'm going to say it anyway. When we found you, when we ran you over with the car, I should have seen right away how special you are.'

Puzzled but attentive, Harry kept his eyes on George. George went on. 'I have no excuse for not realizing that your feelings could be hurt a lot more easily than the rest of you. But I'm a human, and sometimes we make mistakes.' He paused, then said, 'There is a lot we've learned from you, even if it might just be things we've forgotten.'

Harry looked serious for a moment, as if he was going to make a speech back, but then Little Bob yipped at him and they started playing instead.

'Let's get a picture!' Ernie said. Before George could stop him, Ernie was in the den, opening the closet door. All of George's stuffed hunting trophies came tumbling out. Harry was surrounded by glassy-eyed, disembodied animals. He looked sadly down upon them, then raised his eyes to meet George's.

'This he understands,' George said. The funny thing was, he no longer understood himself. The trophies used to make him proud. Now they embarrassed him. Harry growled a soft growl that sounded disappointed. George was disappointed in himself. 'Nancy? Ern? You too, Sarah.'

The family lined up and George filled their arms with dead animals. He carried the ten-point buck himself. To Harry he handed the wolf head. Solemnly Harry took it.

George dug the grave himself. It was the least he could do. After so much tension, the exercise felt good. When the pit was deep enough, the family laid the trophies one by one inside it. George covered them with dirt and packed it down.

'Hey, dad, aren't you supposed to say something at a funeral?' Ernie asked.

'Like what?' Sarah demanded.

'Uh, I don't know,' Ernie said. 'How about, good night, sleep tight, don't let the bedbugs bite?'

'That's disgusting,' Sarah said.

Ernie shrugged. George looked at the grave. 'How about, uh, I'm sorry?' he said. 'Will that do it?' He looked at Harry. Harry responded by gathering the entire family into a giant Bigfoot hug. His scent, garbage and musk, almost knocked them out.

Nancy gripped her nose shut with her fingers. 'Arggh. George, what are we going to do?'

'I think,' George said, 'that Harry needs to take a bath.'

'Oh, no,' Sarah said. 'Not in my bathtub, he's not. Think of the stink. Think of the ring.' She turned to Harry. 'Besides, you're too big.'

'You got any better ideas, Sarah?' George asked.

'I have!' Ernie said. 'How about the Moffitts' swimming pool?'

• Chapter Thirty-three

Ernie wore his swimming trunks under his bathrobe. He was not only the best swimmer in the family, he also had the least sensitive nose. It only made sense for him to be designated bather. Holding Harry's hand, he crept through the low wall of shrubbery that separated the Hendersons' back yard from the Moffitts'. With soap, shampoo and a stack of towels, his mom and Sarah followed.

The yard was dark, but the full moon's reflection floated like a silver coin on the dark surface of the swimming pool. Ernie peeled off his bathrobe and grinned at Harry. 'Let's go swimming,' Ernie said. For a moment, Harry studied Ernie's small, hairless body. 'Okay, so I'm not Arnold Schwarzenegger,' Ernie said. 'But just wait till my next growing spurt.' Then he grabbed his nose and jumped into the pool. When he surfaced, he saw Harry crouched by the edge, watching closely. He seemed relieved whcn Ernie reappeared. 'Come on in,' Ernie urged. 'The water's fine.'

Harry stuck his big toe in the water and withdrew it. He seemed to frown.

'Okay, so it's a little cold,' Ernie said, treading water. 'But you can't tell me they have heated pools where you come from.'

Harry stuck one whole foot in the water, then pulled it out and delicately shook the water from his fur. Nancy joined him at the poolside. 'I don't like cold water either,' she said. 'But you have to take a bath. Come on, Harry. Won't it feel good to be clean?'

'Sissy, sissy. Harry is a sissy,' Ernie taunted from the middle of the pool.

That did it. Imitating Ernie, Harry held his nose and jumped.

A huge geyser rose up when he hit the water. The enormous splash showered Nancy with spray and bits of garbage.

'Yo! A cannonball,' Ernie exclaimed.

His mother shushed him. 'We don't want to wake Irene.'

Cautiously, Sarah stepped to the edge of the pool. 'Mother, he's been down an awfully long time.'

'Sarah's right. Ernie, is Harry all right?'

'I'll check it out.' Ernie dived down under water, searching for Harry. It was too dark to see. He swam near the bottom, feeling for his friend. Suddenly arms closed around him and Ernie felt himself flying upwards. Locked in a bear hug, Ernie and Harry came zooming out of the water. Harry lifted Ernie high above his head. Ernie put his feet on Harry's shoulders and dived back into the water. Harry submerged too. Ernie grabbed his ankle, and Harry gave him a free ride.

When they came up for air, Ernie's mom said, 'Come on, you guys. Stop horsing around. Ernie, you've got work to do.' She held out a family-size bottle of baby shampoo, a giant-size bar of Ivory soap and a toilet brush.

'Aw, mom, do I have to? We were having fun. Besides, the garbage has already come off.' Ernie swatted the water's surface. It was coated with a greasy scum.

'I want him clean, Ernie. And I mean clean.'

Ernie paddled to the edge of the pool. 'Come on, Harry. Fun's over. You've got to have your bath.'

Harry still wanted to play. He stood in the middle of the pool, grinning his Bigfoot grin at Ernie. When Ernie didn't come, Harry used his big hands as scoops. When he splashed, it was like a sudden downpour.

Ernie's mom got soaked. She stood up to her full height, stamped her foot and read the riot act. 'Harry, you come here. Now!'

Harry looked at her for a minute, then obediently dog-paddled to the edge of the pool.

Ernie held up the shampoo. 'Look, "No more tears".' He opened the bottle and started pouring the contents on Harry. One bottle covered his head, shoulders and chest. Ernie bobbed around Harry, massaging in the shampoo, until he worked up a lather that turned Harry's dark fur white. 'You look like the abominable snowman,' Ernie told him. 'Okay, it's time to rinse. You just duck down, like this.'

He demonstrated. Harry thought it was playtime again. He ducked and kept swimming. 'Ernie,' Ernie's mother said, in her sternest voice. Ernie swam after Harry, caught his hand and towed him back to the shallow end. After a few tries, he persuaded Harry to sit on the side of the pool. His mom handed him the Ivory soap. 'Scrub,' she said.

Ernie scrubbed. His mom handed him the toilet brush, and Ernie used it to work the soap through Harry's fur. Harry's nose twitched at the unfamiliar smell. He didn't look too happy. When Ernie had lathered all of Harry, he handed him the bar of soap and pointed at his private parts. 'You do that yourself,' he said.

Harry studied the soap. Then he licked it. He made a face and spat the bubbles out. 'Go ahead,' Ernie said. 'Wash yourself.' He patted his lower belly. 'Down there.' Harry watched Ernie, then imitated him. 'Good boy,' Ernie said.

Sarah was getting impatient. 'Come on, Ernie, we haven't got all night. What if Mrs Moffitt wakes up and sees us?'

'She'll think we're a bad dream, Sarah,' Ernie said. 'Relax.'

'I can't relax,' Sarah said. 'Hurry up.'

Ernie studied Harry and decided he was well scrubbed. 'Okay, boy. Rinse time.' He plunged into the water and Harry followed. They bobbed and fooled around until Ernie's mom made him get out. She handed him a towel, then held another open for Harry. 'Time to get dry,' she said. 'You don't want to catch cold.'

'Mom,' Ernie protested, 'Bigfoots don't catch colds.'

'How do you know?' Sarah asked. 'They probably get terrible colds. Can you imagine? One sneeze would blow the house down. Ugh. How disgusting.'

Harry crawled out of the pool. Ernie's mom tried to wrap a towel around his waist, but it wouldn't reach. 'Maybe you could just shake yourself off,' she suggested. 'That's what Little Bob does.' Mom imitated Little Bob. Harry imitated her. The water flew. Sarah jumped back. 'Yuck.'

'Okay, everybody. Back to the house. It's starting to get light,' Ernie's mom ordered. She took Harry by the hand and marched him towards the hedge. Following in formation, Ernie looked back over his shoulder at the Moffits' pool. 'Yo! The world's biggest bathtub,' he said.

In the kitchen Harry sniffed his fur, the way Little Bob did after a bath, as if he missed his animal smell. Nancy made cocoa for the kids and fed Harry a head of lettuce and a bunch of bananas. He didn't bother to skin them before he wolfed them down.

'Good stuff, huh?' Ernie asked.

Harry replied with a satisfied belch. Nancy surveyed the scene. 'Ernie, you're a mess. Run upstairs and take a quick shower.'

'Mom, I just had a bath.'

'In dirty water. You run along now.'

Ernie headed for the stairs. Harry tried to follow him. 'Oh no, you don't,' Nancy said. 'You wait down here. Let's see what we can find in the refrigerator. I think there's a whole head of cauliflower. Yum.' She led him back to the kitchen.

Harry liked the cauliflower. George got up from his nap on the sofa. 'Harry, you look like a new man,' he said. 'Whoops. A new Bigfoot.'

Ernie took the world's shortest shower. In no time he was back, Sarah's blowdrier in hand. 'Hey, Harry. I bet you'd love the dry look.'

Ernie sat Harry on the kitchen floor and plugged in the drier. When he turned it on, Harry looked puzzled by the warm wind flowing from it. Ernie blew it on him. Harry flinched. 'It's okay, big guy,' Ernie said. 'Watch.' He directed the airstream at his own head. 'See? It doesn't hurt a bit.' He turned it on Harry. Harry leaned back and closed his eyes.

Nancy picked the matted hair out of Little Bob's brush and handed it to Sarah. 'You give him a good brushing. And I,' she held up the toenail clippers, 'am going to do your nails.' She knelt down and started on his feet. Harry opened his eyes for a minute, then decided it didn't hurt and relaxed again. Sarah stopped brushing to get a plastic bag from the drawer. She held it out to her mother. 'Save the clippings,' she advised. 'They're probably worth a lot of money.' Nancy laughed, but she collected the toenail clippings and put them in the bag.

'Look at this,' Ernie said. 'He's a punk rocker.'

Nancy looked. Ernie was drying Harry's hair so that it stood straight up. 'He looks like he's just stuck his big toe into an electric socket.'

The phone rang. Nancy looked to George. He nodded. 'It's okay.'

Nancy picked up the phone. 'You're not going to believe this,' Irene said. 'I don't believe it.'

'Believe what?' Nancy asked, sounding as innocent as she could.

'The pool,' Irene said. 'The pool man came this morning to clean it out and change the filter, like he does every other month. I just told him to go about his business, but pretty soon he's at the back door. "Mrs Moffitt, there's something I think you should see," so I went out with him – and do you know what?'

'What, Irene?' Nancy asked.

'Well, the water looked like a sewer, I mean an absolute sewer, but that's not the half of it. The pool man picked up the net he uses to scoop out leaves and stuff, and it's full of this disgusting big hairy *glop*. So the guy says, "Mrs Moffitt, do you have a cat?" I told him no. "Good," he says, "then it's just a hairball."'

'Amazing,' Nancy said. 'How do you suppose it got in your pool?'

'Beats me,' Irene said. 'The pool man said, "It looks like that big monster that's been running around loose – you know, that Bigfoot thing – had himself a little dip in your pool." What do you think of that?'

'I think it's nice your pool man has a sense of humour,' Nancy said. 'If you ask me, it was kids.'

'Yeah, maybe,' Irene said. 'I wonder.'

'Not my kids, of course,' Nancy said. 'Oop. Kettle's whistling. I've got to turn it off.'

'I think I'm going back to bed,' Irene said. 'Catch you later.'

Nancy waited to laugh until Irene hung up.

• Chapter Thirty-four

The police told their prisoners they could make one phone call. They would be called in alphabetical order. Jacques groaned. That put him near the middle of the list. He moved around the holding pen, looking for an Anderson or a Baker he could swap places with. The best he could do was Gordon, and that cost him ten bucks. It was early morning when he got his shot at the telephone.

Luckily he kept his lawyer's phone numbers, work and home, with him at all times. Jerome was at home but not awake. It took him a while to grasp the situation.

'I'll see what I can do,' Jerome said. 'I should be able to have you released by some time tomorrow morning.'

Jacques growled into the phone, 'You got an ear? I said, get me out of here NOW. Tomorrow's too late.'

His lawyer started to mumble some excuse. The guard was standing there, nonchalant, pretending he wasn't listening, but Jacques knew he was. He cupped his hand over the mouthpiece. 'I know where he is,' he said.

'You know where who is?'

'For chrissake, Jerome. What have I been doing for the last twenty-five years? HIM.'

'I'm afraid I don't quite understand,' his lawyer said.

Jacques looked at the guard, then whispered into the phone, 'Sasquatch. I know where he is.'

'It seems to me I've heard that one before,' Jerome said.

'This time is different. I've got his address.'

'Jacques, you're talking crazy.'

LaFleur exploded. He didn't care who heard. 'Crazy? You want to see crazed? Just let me sit here one more hour and I'll show you crazy. Make something happen. NOW!'

The guard looked at his watch. 'Time's running out.'

'DO IT, JEROME!' LaFleur bellowed before he hung up the phone.

• Chapter Thirty-five

Ernie was a good teacher and Harry a fast learner. He had a gift for mimicry, and even though most human toys and tools were too small for him, his big hands mastered most of them after a few tries. By mid-morning he'd learned how to use taps, how to turn the television on and off, how to vacuum and how to imitate King Kong. Ernie dug out one of Sarah's outgrown Barbie dolls to be Fay Wray and showed Harry how to beat his chest with his fists while yodelling.

Watching them play, George had mixed feelings. He was moved by Harry's innocence and enthusiasm, and the gentleness he showed Ernie. It also troubled him to see a wild creature so easily seduced by the gadgetry of so-called civilized life. George suspected God had not intended Sasquatch to play Atari. He was not at all surprised when Ernie asked if they could keep him. George had been wondering the same thing himself.

'He's a lot more fun than Little Bob, dad, and I can teach him to be a big help around the house. You know how mom's always wishing we had a maid.'

Nan turned from the stove, where she was grilling cheese sandwiches. 'Oh, Ernie. That's just talk. What do I need a maid for when I've got you and Sarah?'

Ernie fixed pleading eyes on George. 'Come on, dad. He's happy here. He likes me. He likes all of us. Even Sarah.'

'I know he does, Ern. And I like him. I really do, but . . .'

'But what?'

Nan said, 'We can't *afford* to keep him, Ernie. Harry needs to live in the forest, where food is free. We'd have to give Safeway a second mortgage on the house.'

'I'll get a paper round,' Ernie said.

Sarah said, 'He's an *animal*, Ernie. He isn't even house-trained.'

'I can train him just like *that*!' Ernie snapped his fingers.

'Lunch,' Nancy called out. 'Time to eat, everybody.'

The family sat down at the table. Harry served himself straight from the refrigerator – a little of this, a little of that, whatever caught his eye. In the silence his crunching and slurping was loud. 'Besides,' Sarah said, 'he has terrible manners.'

'He does not.'

'Next to yours, Ernie, I'll admit his look good. But I wouldn't want to take him to a restaurant,' Sarah said.

Ernie said, 'He could have his own room in the basement. We could put in some rocks and astroturf and stuff so he'd feel right at home.'

George ate his sandwich slowly. He almost wished that Ernie could convince him. When he had finished eating, George turned to his son. 'I know how you feel, but it's impossible. Harry needs to be in a safe place, and that isn't here.'

Sarah flashed Ernie one of her I-told-you-so looks. 'Dad's right.'

George knew he was only half right. 'I just wish I knew where a safe place was,' he said.

After lunch, Nancy took her wounded plants out on to the back porch to see what she could do for them. She'd only been outside a few seconds when Irene called to her over the hedge. 'Yoo-hoo, Nancy. Do you have a second?'

Nancy looked behind her. No Harry in sight. 'Sure, Irenc.'

Her neighbour stepped through the hedge. 'I just need somebody to talk to,' she said. 'This hasn't been easy, with the pool and all. Herb's no help. His latest theory is that a condor flew over and did his business in it.'

Yipping wildly, the neighbourhood dog pack came racing around the house and disappeared around the other side. Nancy had almost got used to them. Faithfully, they followed Harry's movements inside the house.

Irene looked after them. 'Unless it's those crazy dogs. What's wrong with them anyway?'

'Ah, it's just Little Bob,' Nancy said. 'He's quite the ladies' man.'

Inside the kitchen Nancy could hear the ringing of the telephone. 'Oops. There's the phone,' she told Irene. 'I gotta go now.'

George ran through a mental list of all the people he didn't want to talk to. At the moment this included his father, the media and the entire Seattle Police Department. He'd decided not to be in when Harry picked up the receiver and handed it to him. 'Hello?'

'I saw you on television last night, Mr Hen, and I think we should talk. I'm sorry about the –.'

'Who is this?' George asked.

'Do the words "vital facts that could prevent an unnecessary and tragic end for the big fellow" ring a bell?'

The bell rang loudly. 'Yes! Dr Wrightwood?'

'I think we need to talk as soon as possible. You name the time and place.'

'Fine. How about our house? Great. This evening? How about dinner?'

Dr Wrightwood accepted the invitation. George hung up and told Nan they were having company.

• Chapter Thirty-six

When Nancy got home from shopping, the house was a mess again. At least Harry was a help. He carried all her grocery sacks from garage to kitchen in just one trip. When Nancy got inside herself, she threw back her head and bellowed, loudly enough to make Harry stare at her in admiration, 'ER-NIE! SA-RAH! GEORGE! ON THE DOUBLE!'

When the family assembled, she gave them their marching orders. Everything, including themselves, was to be clean, shiny and on its best behaviour no later than six o'clock. Ernie made a face. Nancy grabbed his shirt collar. 'This means you.'

Nancy laid her purchases out on the kitchen counter: five extra-long loaves of French bread, two pounds of fresh spinach, three different kinds of lettuce, a couple of pounds of fresh mushrooms, greens, half a pound of unsalted sunflower seeds, four avocados, half a dozen tomatoes, six bunches of celery, eight baking potatoes, a pound of bean sprouts and, for the humans, an eight-pound sirloin tip roast. It added up to the family food budget for an entire week.

If she got the roast in the oven now, it would be ready in time. As she knelt and felt for the roasting pan, she heard Harry come into the kitchen. Why not? It was his favourite room. Even the television couldn't hold a candle to the refrigerator. When Nancy stood up, Harry was helping himself to a very big handful of bean sprouts. She swatted his hand. 'No snacks. I don't want you to spoil your supper.'

Looking just a little bit ashamed of himself, Harry moved back and watched intently while she unwrapped the roast. The butcher's paper was red with beef blood. Harry sniffed, then wrinkled up his nose in distaste. 'Oh, this,' Nancy said. 'Don't worry. You don't have to eat any.' She went to the cabinet to get salt, pepper and garlic. When she turned back, Harry was holding the roast in his hands. 'Roast,' Nancy said. 'Dinner.'

Harry shook his head from side to side.

'What do you mean, no? You know what that thing cost per pound?'

Quick as he was to learn most things, Harry hadn't quite grasped the concept of money. He obviously didn't care about the price of beef. Palming the roast, he marched out of the kitchen door. Nancy followed in time to see Harry solemnly burying her entrée. He returned to the kitchen, gave her a disapproving look and helped himself to a bunch of celery before he went off to find Ernie. Nancy checked her salad-dressing supply.

By six o'clock the house looked good. The kids looked good. Nancy had found time to shower and put on a pretty dress. George was proud of his family. Now he had to coach Harry. He led him into the den. 'You stay. Stay. Sorry. I mean, you just hang out here, okay? Until I call you.' He turned to his son. 'Ernie, see if you can find something for Harry to do.' The bell rang. 'Good boy,' George said, as he shut them in the den.

Whomever he expected, it was not the person he found on the front porch. 'You,' George stuttered. Better dressed, cleaner shaven, but unmistakably the same, the old man from the museum stood there. He was carrying a large bouquet of flowers.

The old man took off his hat and extended his hand to George. 'Hello, Mr Henderson. I'm Wallace Wrightwood.'

'You're *Doctor* Wrightwood?'

The old doctor gave George a pleasant if slightly guilty smile. 'May I come in?'

George stepped back to let him pass. Nancy appeared. George introduced her. With a flourish, the old man presented his bouquet to Nancy. 'Very pleased to meet you, Mrs Henderson.'

'Likewise. These are beautiful. Thanks. Oh, and this is Sarah and . . .' Nan looked around. 'Where's Ernie?'

Ernie knew better than to tell Harry to sit. Instead he pointed at the armchair. Harry got the idea. He sat down carefully. Ernie flipped through the tape case. 'What do you want to hear?' He picked out a tape. 'How about this? Randy Newman. You're gonna love "Short People".'

Ernie loaded the tape and put the earphones on Harry. His head was so big they almost broke. Ernie punched a button. Harry looked amazed when he heard the music playing in both ears.

'Pretty neat, huh?' Ernie said. 'I gotta go. Company. That's why I'm in this monkey suit.' Maybe that was the wrong thing to say. 'Dressing-up clothes,' he corrected. As he turned towards the door, Ernie saw Harry smile. He was starting to move in time to the music.

George ushered their guest into the living-room. 'By the way,' Dr Wrightwood said, 'I'd be more than happy to buy back the lamp and all the other articles you . . .'

'Don't be silly. Besides, they're buried somewhere and . . .' Ernie appeared in the living-room. 'Ah, here's our Ernie,' George said. 'Meet Dr Wrightwood, son. He's . . .' George stopped talking when he noticed Wrightwood sniffing the air. He'd caught the Bigfoot scent. Ernie grinned so wide George thought his face would break.

'Something sure smells . . .' The doctor paused, looking for the right word. He finished lamely, '. . . good.'

Nancy clapped her hands. 'Dinner! It's almost ready. Why don't we all sit down? George, you settle people in. I want to get these flowers into some water.'

Harry got up. He discovered he could pick up the Walkman and take it with him. He began to explore. On the wall he saw a leaf like the one the male creature had given him to eat. It was in some kind of container, but that was easily broken. Carefully Harry extracted a twenty-dollar bill and popped it in his mouth.

Best dishes, good silver. The table was nicely set. The children sat up straight and kept their hands off the food. George poured wine for the grown-ups. Nancy set Wrightwood's bouquet, prettily arranged, on the table. She nodded graciously to their guest. 'Please, Dr Wrightwood, help yourself.'

Ernie eyed the table. 'Uh, mom, where's the roast?'

George bounced up from his chair. 'Oh, the roast. I'll get it, hon.'

Nancy motioned him to sit. 'The roast is resting in a shallow unmarked grave in the backyard.'

'Too bad he doesn't hate broccoli,' Ernie said.

George passed the French bread to Dr Wrightwood. 'Here. Take lots.' He watched Wrightwood taking stock of their meatless meal. The old man smiled tolerantly.

'Are you folks vegetarians?' he asked.

George smiled back. 'Sometimes,' he told him. 'It depends on the guest.' He piled his own plate high with bread and greenery. For a meat-and-potatoes man, it looked a little bleak. George raised his fork and saluted their guest, then began to eat.

Doc Wrightwood crunched his vegetables. George hoped they wouldn't hurt his dentures. 'Ummm, delicious,' Wrightwood said. His lie was obvious but polite. Nancy acknowledged the compliment with a sceptical nod. Then Wrightwood turned to the kids. 'As you probably know, your dad paid me a visit the other day at my museum,' he said. 'I didn't let him know who I was because, to tell you the truth, I've had it up to here with people who think they've discovered Bigfoot and want to share the secret with me. I used to listen even if I didn't believe them because I believed in *him*.'

Ernie grinned broadly, barely able to stay in his chair. George frowned him a warning. 'Are you saying you don't any more?' he asked.

Having finished the rabbit food, Wrightwood laid his folded napkin beside his plate. 'Will you allow an old man to tell a story? It just might save your lives.'

Nancy nodded encouragement. 'If you put it that way,' she said.

'When I was younger,' Doc said, 'I used to have a good job working as a lab scientist. Life was great. I was in love with a set of curves named Lee Ann.' He looked at Nancy. 'I thought of her about half an hour ago when I met a certain somebody.'

Nancy blushed prettily.

Doc went on. 'Anyway, we were going to get hitched, have us a couple of little tax exemptions . . .' Now he looked at Sarah and Ernie. 'A boy and a girl, if we had any say in it.' His eyes got a faraway look. 'But something happened on a hunting trip darned near fifty years ago that let the air out of everything.'

Poor old guy. George wanted to show his sympathy. 'She was killed?' he asked.

Wrightwood shot George a sharp glance. 'Hell, no, she wasn't killed. She married a Buick dealer from Portland and now she's got more money than God.'

Nancy spoke for them all when she said, 'I'm afraid I'm lost.'

'Yeah. I don't get it,' Ernie echoed.

'Listen,' Wrightwood said. 'Here's what happened. I went out for a walk in the woods alone. It was late afternoon, just before sunset. I heard a rustle behind me, loud – like a bear or a man would make. Then I smelled something that made my eyes water and my lungs smoke.'

'Tell us about it,' Sarah said.

The den door opened quietly behind Wrightwood. Just as quietly, Harry entered the room. George willed himself to keep a poker face. It was hard.

'What do you think it was?' Ernie asked Wrightwood.

Good boy, George thought.

'The honest truth is, I don't know. By the time I turned around, all I saw was a flash of fur. On the ground there was a footprint – a big footprint, just like a man's, only three times the size.' Wrightwood paused.

'Please, Doctor,' Nancy said. 'Finish your story.'

'Well . . . I was hooked from that moment on.'

Harry was on his way across the living-room, but something in Wrightwood's voice caught his attention. He stopped moving and stared at the old man.

'I started spending all the time I could spare searching for the beast. Then I spent time I couldn't spare. That's how I lost Lee Ann, then my job, then my friends.'

'That's the saddest story I've ever heard,' Sarah said. There were real tears in her eyes. George smiled fondly. There was more to his daughter than Michael Jackson and styling gel after all.

'Well, I didn't tell it so you could cry into your bean sprouts or whatever this is, darlin',' Doc Wrightwood said gruffly. 'I told it so your father here wouldn't make the same mistake.' He looked at George. 'You're holding good cards here. Don't fold 'em.'

George said, 'I appreciate that, Doctor. But there's a big difference between you and me.'

The old man shook his head. 'Not as big as you think.'

Harry wandered into the dining-room in search of food. He stood right behind Dr Wrightwood, eyeing the spinach. George tried to contain his smile. 'Maybe even bigger,' he said.

'Don't kid yourself, Mr Henderson. I saw you on the boob tube last night, and I remember what you said when you came into my shop. "Bigfoot can come and live with us. We'll accept responsibility."' Wrightwood rasped a cynical laugh. 'Can you imagine what a Bigfoot would do to your home?'

Fighting giggles, the family looked around at the fresh plaster, the patched furniture. Nancy opened her eyes wide, all innocence, and nodded no.

'Well, I can,' Dr Wrightwood said. 'You're good people. I'm going to say this once, and I'm going to say it simple, and I hope to God for your sakes that you all listen.' Wrightwood's voice rose and his face grew red. 'THERE ARE NO ABOMINABLE SNOWMEN, THERE ARE NO SASQUATCHES AND THERE ARE NO BIGFEET.'

Harry stood behind the doctor, about to snatch the salad. The family's faces melted into smiles. Ernie giggled. The doctor looked confused. 'Am I missing something?'

George looked up at Harry. 'Yes, Doc. For too long.'

The old man swivelled in his chair, following the direction of George's gaze. He found himself staring at Harry's lower abdomen. George watched the double-take, how Doc's eyes travelled, up, up, up, until they reached Harry's. The doctor's amazement met Harry's gentle curiosity. They stared at each other for a long moment.

The doctor stood up, small beside the Sasquatch whose existence he had just denied. 'Lordy . . . Lord . . . God!'

'Dr Wrightwood, say hello to Harry.'

The old man could barely speak. His words came as slowly as a two-year-old's. 'Hello, Harry.' Wrightwood looked Harry up and down, down and up, his smile rising like the sun on a clear morning. Then he opened up his mouth and yelped. 'YAH . . . HOOOOO!'

Harry was interested in the old man who stood below him, watching his every move. Harry looked Wrightwood in the eye with compassion in his curiosity.

Nancy leaned close to the old man and whispered. 'He's pretty smart. George even taught him to sit.'

Wrightwood looked astonished. *'Sit?'* he repeated.

Harry sat. The chair couldn't take it. He sat on the floor. It made him just the right height for the dining-room table.

'We're still perfecting it,' George said.

Nancy filled a salad plate for Harry. 'What kind of dressing do you want?' she asked, then pushed the salad plate aside and took Wrightwood's bouquet from the centre of the table. She set it in front of Harry. 'What the heck? Enjoy.'

Harry was on his best behaviour. Instead of stuffing the whole arrangement in his mouth at once, he delicately plucked the blossoms off, one by one, and savoured them. He even chewed with his mouth closed.

'And he lives here with you?' Doc Wrightwood asked.

'It's only temporary,' Sarah said.

• Chapter Thirty-seven

It was night before Jerome showed up at the jail. All day Jacques had been pacing like a caged animal, which was exactly what he was. After a while he became accustomed to his own ripe garbage smell, but his fellow prisoners continued to give him a wide berth.

Jerome was turned out like the sissy Jacques had always suspected he was – three-piece suit, dark tie and shiny shoes. He gave his disgruntled client a slick, professional smile. 'How are you?'

'How do you think I am?' Jacques growled. 'Am I free to go?'

'Afraid not, LaFleur.' Jerome deliberated. 'If I call in a favour, I might be able to get you out some time tonight.'

It was all Jacques could do not to rip the bars off the holding pen. 'Some time tonight! It might be too late already –'

'But I'm going to need a damn good reason,' Jerome informed him.

The man's head was made of wood. He had straw between his ears. It was probably a requirement to get into law school these days. Jacques roared at his lawyer. '*Sacré bleu!* I'm talking about bagging a Sasquatch!'

'Great,' Jerome said. 'Terrific, LaFleur. That ought to cut a lot of ice with the judge.'

Jacques reached between the bars and grabbed his attorney's necktie. 'GET ME OUT OF HERE . . .' He dropped his voice. 'Or we'll see what I can cut besides ice.' Jacques let go of the lawyer's tie.

Jerome looked flustered. 'You're a wild man, LaFleur. But I'll see what I can do.' The lawyer straightened his tie.

'You do understand that there's an extra charge for night work?'

'Extortionist!' Jacques spat. Then he said, 'I don't care what it costs. Just get me out.'

• Chapter Thirty-eight

'Hey! Watch this.' Ernie tugged at Doc Wrightwood's sleeve. 'Harry wants to show you how he can play "Space Invaders".'

'Ernie,' his dad warned. 'The doctor and I have important things to talk about.'

'Please, dad . . .'

Doc put his hand on Ernie's shoulder. 'Show me. This I've got to see.' He turned to Ernie's dad. 'We've got all night, haven't we?'

What could Dad say? Ernie took Wrightwood by the hand and led him to the living-room, where Harry was waiting for them in front of the TV. Ernie turned on the game and installed the joysticks in Harry's giant hand. Animated blips of spaceships cruised across the television screen. 'Blast 'em, Harry!' Ernie urged. 'You can do it, boy.'

With grave concentration Harry peered at the screen, his whole head following the moving graphics.

'Shoot! Now!'

Blam! Harry exploded an alien rocket.

'All right!' Ernie hugged him. They watched as Harry bagged two more invaders. 'He's got great reflexes,' Ernie told Doc. 'It took him a while to figure out what you're supposed to do, but once he caught on, POW!'

'Bigfoot Shoots Spacemen,' Doc said. 'Now there's a headline for you.'

'I wish he could join my soccer team,' Ernie said. 'Harry would make a great goalie. I bet nothing would get by him.' Ernie liked the old guy his dad had invited home for dinner. He sort of wished they could keep him too. Grandpa Henderson was too busy to spend any time with Ernie, and their other grandparents lived in Arizona now. They'd moved there for the sunshine, and Ernie hardly ever got to see them. Maybe the family could adopt Doc Wrightwood.

'Ernie, Harry, come over here. Now! It's time for dessert. Your dad's built a fire in the fireplace.' Mom was on the warpath again.

Ernie was torn between wanting to finish the game, and keep Doc to himself, and his mother's chocolate pie. She'd made one and hidden it in the dishwasher so Harry wouldn't find it on one of his refrigerator raids.

'Ernie!' his dad called.

Doc Wrightwood put his hand on Ernie's shoulder. 'What do you say we see what's for dessert?' His voice dropped to a whisper. 'It's got to be better than dinner.'

'Yo. Come on, Harry. I think you're really gonna like this.'

They joined the family at the coffee table in front of the fireplace. Ernie counted only three slices of chocolate pie. 'Where's ours?' he asked.

'In the kitchen,' Mom said. 'Your dad and Doctor Wrightwood need to talk, Ernie. You kids take Harry out of the way and eat your dessert. Then I want you to get on with your homework.'

'The kitchen?' Ernie couldn't believe they were sending him to the kitchen just when things were getting interesting.

'Be glad I'm not making you do the dishes,' Mom said.

Doc Wrightwood gave his mother a winning smile. 'With all due respect, Mrs Henderson – Nancy – why not let the boy stay? He might learn something.'

'All right!' Ernie hollered.

The doctor turned to him. 'And you, Ernie, you have to promise to be quiet and not interrupt.' His voice was stern.

'I promise,' Ernie said.

Both he and Doc looked at his mom. She nodded. 'Okay, you can stay. As long as you're quiet.'

Doc settled on the sofa and patted the cushion beside him. 'You sit by me, where I can keep an eye on you.' Ernie plopped down. Harry sat with his back against the wall. Sarah helped Mom serve pie and coffee. Harry gulped his pie and held out his plate for more. Mom said, 'You wait until everyone else is done, Harry.' The Bigfoot licked the last crumbs off his finger fur and sighed.

'How can I help you, George?' Doc asked Dad.

'I want to do the right thing,' Dad said, 'but it's not always easy to figure out just what that is.'

Doc nodded. 'That's the human condition, George. If we all agreed on what was right, well, we'd never disagree with each other. No fights. No wars.' The old man looked at Harry. 'I can't help wondering what *he* knows.'

'He knows how to vacuum,' Ernie said. 'I taught him how this afternoon.'

'Ernie, you promised,' Sarah said.

'I know, but . . .'

Doc's glare shut Ernie up. 'What he knows about living,' Doc went on. 'Think about it. Sasquatch is much bigger and more powerful than man. He may well be equally intelligent. But you haven't seen him building any bombs or starting any wars. In fact, he's lived peacefully in the forest for centuries, keeping out of sight while we've brought *our* race, and his, to the brink of disaster.' Suddenly Doc turned to Sarah. 'Why do you think that is?'

Sarah looked flustered. She played with her napkin. 'Uh, maybe because he doesn't eat meat? Or watch television?'

Doc smiled at her. 'Very good, Sarah.' Ernie was glad Doc hadn't put him on the spot. 'The fact is, we don't know why. It would sure be interesting to find out. It might even be important.'

'That's what I've been thinking, Doc. There's so much Harry could teach us about . . . well, a lot of things. But I'm not exactly sure who's willing to learn,' Dad said.

'Just so,' Doc said.

Mom spoke up. 'All this stuff you read about what they do to laboratory animals,' she said. 'It makes my blood run cold. What if they thought of Harry as just another dumb animal? We did at first.'

'On the other hand,' Dad said, 'what if Harry could help humans discover something they need to know, like a cure for cancer or where we all came from?'

Doc nodded. 'Even scientists, in their enthusiasm, sometimes overlook the obvious. And don't forget, Harry is a very *valuable* find. Imagine how much Ringling Brothers would pay to put him in the circus. Imagine what collectors would pay to own the only known stuffed Bigfoot.'

Ernie looked at Harry. His big brow was wrinkled, as if he had a headache. He followed the conversation, keeping his eyes on the person who spoke. Ernie wondered if he understood. If he did, he had every reason to feel bad. Quietly, he got up from the sofa and slipped into the kitchen. There was about a third of the chocolate pie left. Ernie looked longingly at it, then took it in to Harry. 'Here. This is for you.' Harry stuck one big finger into the chocolate filling and offered it to Ernie. Ernie licked the chocolate off. 'Thanks, Harry. Don't you worry. You can trust these guys.' He nodded at his dad and Doc Wrightwood. 'They'll figure out what's best.'

Ernie sat back down beside the doctor and tried to follow the conversation. His eyes were getting heavy. He yawned.

George poured his heart out to Dr Wrightwood. He told him all the thoughts and questions that had been running around his head for days. One by one, the kids conked out, Ernie first, then Sarah. Harry, in his corner, was starting to look drowsy. His yawns were as big as caves.

'Poor Harry,' Nan said. 'You've had a big day. The trouble is, I don't know quite where to put you to bed.' She got up from her armchair and stood beside Harry, patting his head.

'Harry's a woodland creature, you know,' Doc said. 'If you could build him some kind of nest, he'd probably feel right at home.'

George thought a minute. 'Say, Nan, how about those branches we trimmed from the trees in the yard? I haven't had a chance to take them to the dump yet.' He looked at Doc. 'We've got a little behind with household maintenance lately.'

'They're behind the garage,' Nan said. She took Harry's hand. 'Come on, buddy. Let's make your bed.'

'You want help, Nan?' George offered.

'No, you two talk. Harry and I can manage,' she said. A few minutes later, they were back, their arms full of branches. Harry looked questioningly at Nancy. She pointed to a corner near the fireplace. 'How about over there?' Harry carried his branches to the corner and started to build his nest. Nancy laid her armload beside his.

'I don't know,' George told the doctor, 'after people caught on that Bigfoot was in town, they sort of went crazy. And when I saw all those bozos, armed to the teeth and eager to kill, well . . .' George shook his head. 'Not ten days ago, I was just like them. Now, that's a sobering thought.'

Doc nodded thoughtfully.

'The point is, Doc, if I thought everybody, I mean like, well, mankind in general would learn what I have in the last week just from having Harry around, I wouldn't hesitate . . . But the way I see it, even the scientific community is gonna poke and prod him until he hates every man he sees, including you and me.'

Doc looked at Harry, peacefully reclining in his bed of boughs. 'It's gonna be harder letting him go than it was finding him.'

Nancy nodded. 'We know.'

'A safe place is the only answer,' George said.

Doc Wrightwood stroked his chin. 'I might just know one. But we'll never be able to find it at night.'

George leaned forward. 'Then you'll help us?'

'In every way I possibly can.'

'Thank you,' George said. 'We'll leave first thing in the morning.' Stretching his arms, he stood up. Gently, Nan roused the kids and sent them off to bed. Harry curled up in his nest of branches. George was about to offer their visitor the guest room when Wrightwood got up, stretched too and headed out of the front door without so much as a goodbye.

Nancy looked as confused as George felt. 'What an odd man. No goodbyes, nothing.'

'God,' George said, 'I don't even know what time he's coming back.'

A few minutes later, they heard the door knob rattle. A knock. 'What the . . . ?' George opened the door. Wrightwood stood there with his camping gear, knapsack in one hand, a battered sleeping bag under his arm. The old man nodded at George and Nancy, then proceeded to unfurl his bedroll in the corner, right next to Harry's nest. Fully dressed, he climbed inside. 'Time to catch some zzz's. Goodnight, all,' Wrightwood said.

'Goodnight, Doctor. Goodnight, Harry.' George switched off the living-room light and followed his wife upstairs. With Harry safe and Wrightwood by his side, George was sure he would sleep soundly.

• Chapter Thirty-nine

'Okay, you creeps! Wake up. It's time to go.'

The voice of the police guard interrupted LaFleur's dreams of revenge. He woke on the hard floor of the holding pen. Around him his cellmates sat up, cursing.

'You've been bailed out, all of you,' the cop hollered. 'Get a move-on.'

Jacques rose slowly to his feet, stiff from two nights of confinement. His fellow prisoners, most of them much younger than he, beat him through the narrow door. Riff-raff, all of them. Thirty-six hours in their company had only confirmed LaFleur's disdain for them. He elbowed his way through their ranks into the lobby of the police station. His lawyer, Jerome, was flattened against the far wall to avoid being trampled in the stampede to freedom.

LaFleur confronted Jerome. 'Some lawyer you are. Where have you been?'

His lawyer shrugged. 'Nothing I could do. They weren't releasing anybody till they processed all the guns. There were a *lot* of guns.' Jerome reeled backwards, away from his client. 'Whew! You stink. You sure could use a bath.'

LaFleur had never had much use for lawyers, including his own, or for the stupid games they played. 'What? And blow my cover?' he said. He left his attorney gaping after him, trying to figure out just what *that* meant, and strode into the street.

• Chapter Forty

The family learned something about Harry that night. He snored. HARRY SNORED BIG SNORES. The house reverberated with them.

Doc Wrightwood, who slept like the dead, slept through them.

Sarah went to the bathroom and stuffed wads of surgical cotton in her ears.

George and Nancy put their pillows over their heads.

Ernie took direct action. When his dad snored, his mom just poked him until he rolled over on to his side and stopped. Ernie figured the same might work with Harry. He grabbed his teddy bear, Max, and padded downstairs.

Sure enough, Harry was sleeping on his back. Carefully Ernie stepped over Doc Wrightwood in his sleeping bag and lay down next to Harry. The bed was kind of itchy, with all those leaves. Ernie stuck his elbow in Harry's ribs. The rhythm of his snoring changed a little, but it didn't stop. Ernie poked again. Harry was out like a light. Ernie got to his knees and tried to roll Harry over, but he didn't budge. Finally he found the solution. He dug his fingers into the thick hair over Harry's ribcage and tickled for all he was worth. It worked. Harry wrapped his arms around himself, turned over on his side and curled up in a ball. No more snoring. Ernie snuggled in beside him and fell asleep.

Screams shattered the early-morning quiet.

Ernie sat up. Doc Wrightwood opened his eyes and peered at the unfamiliar surroundings. Harry did nothing. He wasn't there. 'My God, he's gone,' Doc said.

George and Nancy woke face to startled face. In unison, they jumped out of bed and ran to the bedroom window. Irene. She was waving her arms and hollering at her gardener, Mr Kimchee. George opened the bedroom window. They both leaned out to listen, which wasn't hard. Irene was yelling at the top of her lungs.

'You killed them!' She was pointing at her prize rose bushes. Yesterday they had been covered with lush blooms. Now they were naked.

'No, no,' the gardener protested. 'Not me. Maybe it was Pig Foot.'

'What's Pig Foot? Oh, my precious babies! What kind of Japanese gardener can't even take care of roses? That should be one of the first things you learn in Japan.'

'I am Korean,' Mr Kimchee said.

'Don't try to worm your way out of this by changing your nationality, you . . . you . . .'

The little gardener stood right up to Irene. 'I quit,' he announced. He turned on his heel and marched towards his truck, parked in the alley.

Irene screamed after him. 'Come back here, you no-good rose killer!'

Mr Kimchee did not turn back. Shaking his head, he climbed into the cab of his pick-up.

Chuckling softly, George closed the windows.

Mrs Moffitt's screams penetrated the cotton Sarah had stuffed in her ears. She pulled it out and listened to their neighbour. Sarah wondered what had her so upset this time. Pale sunshine crept through the curtains. Sarah sat up on her elbows. Her bedside clock said it was a few minutes before six.

Without a sound, her bedroom door swung open. Harry crept in. On his arm he carried Mom's wicker basket. It overflowed with roses, beautiful roses, all in full bloom. Walking softly, Harry approached Sarah's bed. He took a red rose from his basket and held it out to her.

Sarah took the rose and buried her nose in its soft petals, enjoying the perfume. 'It's beautiful,' she said. 'Thank you.' Sarah looked up from the rose blossom. 'I'm sorry I yelled at you, Harry.'

Harry seemed to have forgiven her for her lecture and all the remarks about his smell. He took another rose, a yellow one, from the basket, smelled it briefly, then ate the flower.

'Don't swallow the thorns,' Sarah warned him.

• Chapter Forty-one

Having been bailed out himself, Jacques found he had to bail out his power wagon too. The cops had impounded it. It took his last dime to get his car back. Once he had, he headed one more time for the home of the mysterious George Henderson. There would be no mistakes this time.

Well, not many. It was a mistake to take the freeway. The entire first shift at Boeing was on its way to work. LaFleur was stuck in the procession turtling its way towards factories and engineering offices. Leaning on his horn didn't make traffic move faster, but it did relieve some of his frustration. Soon other drivers were honking back at him. A loud wail rose from the freeway.

At last he arrived in the Hendersons' neighbourhood. LaFleur parked across the street and took his rifle, also ransomed from the city authorities, from its rack in the rear window. No, better not show all his cards right off. He covered the rifle with a blanket and climbed out of the cab.

Damn! Wally Wrightwood's battered van sat in the Hendersons' driveway. The old fool had got here before him. As LaFleur stood there, a motley pack of dogs ran full speed around the side of the Hendersons' home. They almost knocked him over. Seconds later they were gone. Stealthily Jacques approached the house.

The back was safest. No sense in letting neighbours spot him snooping and call the cops. Jacques had had more than enough of the police recently. He flattened himself against the house and moved cautiously towards the rear. Something colourful, perhaps significant, caught his eye. He stooped and picked up a broken rose blossom. Another lay beside it, and another. LaFleur examined them, then tossed them, all but one, away.

Irene returned from her early-morning foray to the all-night grocery. She wasn't really going to start over-eating again – she'd only bought enough goodies to soothe her frayed nerves. She deserved a sugar fix. It wasn't every day that some villain stole your whole crop of prize roses, after all. Irene began to stuff her purchases – sweets, chocolates, biscuits – into the blender. She hit the whizzer and turned them all into one giant sucrose cocktail. Straight out of the shaker she took a long swallow and immediately felt the welcome rush. *Aaaaahhhhh!!!*

Irene was about to take another mouthful when the flicker of something past the window caught her eye. She pulled back the curtain in time to see the same ruffian who'd turned up on Nancy's doorstep a few days before sneaking past with a handful of roses. *Her roses.*

So it wasn't Mr Kimchee, after all. Poor man. She'd have to call him later to apologize. Now she was going to catch a thief. In the utensil drawer she found the battery-operated carving knife she'd given Herb two Christmases ago, took another long swig of her calorie cocktail and prepared to confront the vicious brutalizer of her roses.

Between them, the family and their guests put away a dozen eggs and a whole loaf of raisin bread, toasted, while Doc and George discussed the safe place for Harry. Wrightwood pushed his empty plate aside. 'Sure would be a dream come true if we could keep him.'

'You know what they say . . . the best things in life are supposed to be free.'

'You make that up?' Doc asked.

George realized he was being teased. Profundity had never been his strong suit. He smiled. 'No. But I'm starting to believe it.' Harry picked up the discarded breakfast plates and one by one licked them clean with his tongue, then passed them to Nancy at the dishwasher. Suddenly something outside the window caught his attention. He tensed.

LaFleur crept up to what he guessed must be the kitchen window. The window was covered, but a thin pencil of space showed between the curtains. Jacques moved closer and pressed one eye against the glass.

'Hold it right there, mister,' a female voice behind him said.

LaFleur spun around to find a wild-eyed woman in curlers and a flowered housecoat. She waved a knife at him. 'One false move and I'll prune your plant, fella. And I am talking *nip it in the bud.*'

LaFleur was an experienced tracker. He had encountered many dangers in the woods, but this crazed housewife struck fear into his heart.

Conversation stopped when they heard Irene's voice. It sounded as if it came from just outside the kitchen window. Harry stood by the sink, his head cocked, listening. Then he growled, a low grumble deep in his throat, and reached out his long arm to part the curtains. Pressing his face against the window, Harry bared his teeth and roared.

Irene was relieved when she saw her neighbours' curtains open. They would see she needed help. She raised her face to the window, expecting to see George or Nancy there. A snarling monster stared back at her. Irene threw back her head and screamed. The neighbourhood dog pack gathered, leaping, at her ankles and bayed at the Hendersons' window.

Doc Wrightwood pulled Harry aside and looked out of the window. He drew the curtains closed. 'LaFleur!' he said.

Harry strained towards the window, teeth bared, growling. George held his arm, talking softly. 'Easy now, Harry. It's okay, boy.' He could feel the power tensed in the big arm.

Doc Wrightwood headed for the kitchen door. 'I'll go out and talk to Jock now, and I'll explain later. You keep our friend in here. He'll be perfectly safe as long as he's inside.'

With one swift thrust Harry pulled away from George. Without stopping to open it, he smashed through the kitchen door and into the yard. The door splintered with a thunderous crash.

Irene jumped at the sound of a terrible commotion. Her adversary took advantage of her surprise and reached out to take the knife away from her. Irene felt for the switch and turned her weapon on. She brandished it at the rose-killer.

Then the monster appeared again. No doubt about it – a genuine gigantic, snarling, growling, ANGRY monster appeared in the Hendersons' back yard. Paralysed by fear, Irene watched as the monster stilled the yapping dogs with one stern glance, then silently urged them to turn on the rose thief. Teeth bared, they rushed to do his bidding. The creep was trapped.

Doc couldn't help smiling when he found his old antagonist surrounded by the pooch patrol.

'It's not fair!' LaFleur shouted. 'You gave up the search. He should be *mine*.'

To LaFleur Doc said, 'He should be *free*.' To George he said, 'What do you say we hit the road? We'll take my van.'

'Sounds good,' George said. 'Come on, everybody. Let's go!'

Wrightwood, the Hendersons and Harry all ran for the van. The family scrambled in, and Doc raced the engine while Harry's canine disciples held LaFleur at bay on the lawn. Little Bob leapt through Nancy's open window on to her lap. Harry sat up and customized Doc Wrightwood's van with a Bigfoot dome. Squealing the tyres, Doc backed out of the driveway.

'All right!' Ernie said.

Doc stopped the van directly across the street. He opened his door and hopped out. 'You drive, George.'

'What's he doing?' Nancy asked. 'Isn't he coming with us?'

Ernie stared, wide-eyed, out of the window. 'Look at that,' he said. The family looked. Doc was plunging his pocket knife deep into the tyres of LaFleur's pick-up. They deflated on the spot. When LaFleur's truck was effectively crippled, Doc hopped in the back with Harry and George sped away.

LaFleur watched his tyres melt slowly into the street. There was nothing he could do until the pack of dogs took off after Wrightwood's van. 'Damn you, Wally! This isn't over yet,' LaFleur shouted after them. He looked wildly around. To change his tyres would take an hour. Besides, he only had one spare. Then his eyes lit on the Hendersons' station wagon in the garage. It looked like a wreck, but if it ran, Jacques was prepared to borrow it. He grabbed his rifle from the pick-up, then climbed into the station wagon. Someone had obligingly left the keys in the ignition.

Jacques roared away.

Irene watched him go. So the rose thief was a car thief too. She regretted not carving him up like a leg of lamb. Irene raised her fist and shook it at the retreating station wagon. 'You won't get away with this, you creep!' she yelled. 'I've got your registration number!'

• Chapter Forty-two

Doc's van did fine at thirty, but once George put it into third gear, the whole rig shuddered. 'Uh, what year did you say this thing was, Doc?' George called over his shoulder.

'Tell the truth, I don't quite remember. Let's see . . . I think I bought her back in '48. Or was it '50?'

'Jeez,' Ernie said. 'Your van is three times older than me.'

'Something like that,' Doc said. 'Don't worry, George. There's life in the old girl yet.'

George hoped so. They were hitting Highway 99, bound for the interstate. Once they hit a fast road, the dogs thought better of following. In the mirror George watched them, one by one, give up the chase. A ragged file of panting dogs lined the emergency lane behind them. 'Well, we lost the mutts,' he told them. 'Hope they can find their way home.'

Ernie looked back as the van sped on. He spotted a station wagon with two major head wounds gaining on them from behind. 'Uh-oh. Don't look now, but I think we're being followed by our own car.'

A glance in the wing mirror confirmed it. The station wagon zipped from lane to lane, barely escaping collisions on all sides. From the rear, Harry growled at it. George wasn't sure whether he was reacting to the wagon or to LaFleur.

Traffic slowed in front of him, and George checked to see if it was safe to manoeuvre left. As he pulled parallel to the car in the next lane, a small boy in the passenger seat spotted Harry in the van. His mother, driving, turned her head for a quick look and almost hit them broadside. George wrestled with the steering wheel, escaping with a scratch.

'All right, dad!' Ernie cheered. 'You're driving like an escaped psycho.'

The I-5 South entrance appeared on their right, and George took it before he realized the freeway was having one of its bad days. Too many cars, too little road. Traffic was moving at about forty slowing steadily. He was no sooner installed in the slow lane than a police siren wailed behind him. Its red and blue lights flashed and spun, growing larger in the rearview mirror. Obediently the cars in George's lane pulled over to yield the right of way.

'Is he after us, dad?' Sarah asked.

'I'm not sure.'

They waited in silence as the police car came alongside and sped by. 'Whew!' Ernie said. 'That was a close one.' The impromptu lane the cop car had formed closed up again. They were even more stuck than before. Behind them their station wagon bounced out of the slow lane on to the shoulder and picked up speed.

'Hey! What's he doing to my car?'

Everyone in the van turned to watch LaFleur and the station wagon jolt closer. Traffic moved at a snail's pace. There was no escape – that is, until Harry stuck his head out the window and let fly with an ear-splitting roar.

'Wow, dad,' Ernie said, 'he sounds just like a cop car.' Ernie was right. Their fellow motorists were convinced. Again they pulled aside, creating a temporary fast lane for the police. 'Keep it up, Harry,' George yelled as he pulled into the opening and accelerated hard. The van stalled for an instant, then blasted out a massive backfire that left most of the exhaust system lying in the road. A trail of blue-white smoke poured from the rear end as they raced up the freeway. 'Eat that, Jocko,' Doc called out of his window as traffic filled in behind them.

South of the city the traffic eased and the van picked up speed. There was no sign of the station wagon behind them when they hit the Mount Rainier turn-off just north of Tacoma. 'We did it!' George exclaimed. 'That sucker's history.'

'Don't kid yourself,' Doc said. 'This is the part he's good at.'

*

LaFleur had still not caught up by the time Doc directed them off the main highway on to a logging road. 'Home and dry, Doc,' George said hopefully. 'Aren't we?'

'Don't count on it,' Wrightwood said. 'Remember, I've known Jock for thirty years, more or less. There's lots of things you can call him, but quitter's not one of them.'

'Step on it, dad,' Ernie advised.

'I am,' George said. He was almost used to the shudder by now.

Nancy started the family singing 'Ninety-Nine Bottles of Beer on the Wall' to ease the tension. Harry growled along, keeping time. He seemed to enjoy the song.

When they got down to fifty-one bottles of beer on the wall, Doc hollered, 'Stop! Stop! We just passed it.' George slammed on the brakes and backed up.

'I always miss the turn-off. It's real hard to spot,' Doc said.

George said, 'That's a good sign.'

Doc peered out of the window. 'Here it is,' he said. The van bounced into the forest.

Ernie pointed. 'Look at that. It's already snowed up here.'

'Yeah, it's freezing,' Sarah said.

George turned on the heater, which, amazingly enough, still worked.

'Forty-six bottles of beer on the wall,' the family chorus chirped.

'Thirty-nine bottles of beer.'

At twenty-eight bottles Doc told them they were there. The family piled out of the van. 'How you wanna handle this, George?' Doc asked.

George sighed. 'We've got to get Harry off into the woods, away from LaFleur. And us.' He turned to Harry. The Bigfoot's face was sad. George moved closer. 'You understand, Harry? You've got to go back to where you belong. You're in danger here.'

Abruptly Harry's eyes, which had been fixed on George's, rose. Seconds later the humans too picked up the sound. It was the station wagon. The family converged on Harry, urging him to run, shoo, scat. George looked over his shoulder, then turned back to Harry. 'Go, Harry! Run!' He pointed back down the road. 'Danger! LaFleur! Hunter!'

Harry understood danger. He wanted to protect them from it. He stood his ground and growled. Then he started down the road himself. George planted a restraining hand on Harry's chest. 'No. Please.'

It was hopeless. Not only was Harry huge, he was hugely loyal. George hardened his heart and his expression. 'Get out of here. Can't you see we don't want you any more?' he yelled at Harry. 'Go back to where you came from.'

Slowly Harry looked at the faces of the family, one by one.

'Leave us alone!' George hollered. Then he slapped Harry squarely across the face. Harry's immediate response was anger. George watched as it melted into a deep sadness. George's heart ached inside him. 'Go! Go!' he screamed at his friend.

Harry stepped back from George, then turned and walked towards the woods. After a few steps he turned back to George. His face was sad and hopeful.

George turned his back on Harry. Under his breath, his voice breaking, he whispered, 'Goodbye, my friend.'

In silence the family watched Harry disappear among the trees. Ernie sniffed loudly. Nancy looked down and saw his tears. Her own were fighting to come out. 'Ernie, stop that right now.' Neither she nor Ernie could stop. They cried. George hugged them both.

Sarah was dry-eyed but her face was sad. She said what everyone else was thinking. 'We'll never see him again, will we?'

Ernie pulled out of his father's embrace. His face brightened. 'Sure we will. We can just follow the footprints.' He pointed at the snow around them.

'Oh, my God,' George said.

'The footprints,' Doc said.

Ernie said, 'Yeah, right there. See? They're clear as a bell.'

And so they were.

• Chapter Forty-three

LaFleur never doubted he would find them, not with that blue-white smoke to guide him. Even when it faded from sight, its carbon monoxide stench lingered in the air. Jacques had an educated nose. He saluted the decrepitude of Wally Wrightwood's ancient van.

In the station wagon he followed them off I-5, at the Mount Rainier turn-off, then on to a smaller logging road, the one where he'd first found evidence of the accident. They were returning to the scene of the crime. Time to be alert. His eyes combed the dense forest on either side of the road. Windows down, he sniffed the air as he drove.

Just as expected, the smoke showed him the way. He switched back on to a turn-off he'd never seen before. Here tyre marks on the wet ground collaborated with the smoke. He followed until he found the place where they'd stopped.

Grabbing his rifle, Jacques climbed out of the car. A confusion of human tracks and – yes, a set of Bigfoot prints in the snow. Clear as a map, they led him into the forest. He cocked his gun.

About a hundred yards into the trees LaFleur detected something curious – another set of Bigfoot prints crossed those he followed. A meeting? A welcome home? The thought of more than one Sasquatch exhilarated him. He followed the second set of tracks until they dead-ended in a dry patch.

Looking around, he spotted a third set of giant footprints. Could there be three? He followed closely. Another hundred yards, and one set of tracks branched into two. Two multiplied to four. They came and went in all directions.

LaFleur took off his hat and scratched his head. His brain was reeling. Bigfoot musk teased his nose.

'It's a goddam herd,' the tracker said. He was so intent on mayhem he never thought to be afraid.

Harry reclined at the top of a tall cedar. It was good to be home. When he stretched out his arms, the forest birds came to roost on them. The birds tittered in his ears. They seemed glad to have him back.

From his treetop Harry could just see his friends in the distance, still playing their strange game. With peculiar, heavy tools tied to their feet, they were wandering this way and that through the woods. Harry had picked a place to rest where he could keep an eye on them.

The tracks were everywhere. Usually Jacques could read animal prints like a book, but this tale had no plot. No sooner did he run one way, thinking he'd made sense of it at last, than the tracks stopped, or separated, or simply disappeared. His grip on reality was beginning to slip. Would Bigfoot drive him mad?

Wait! Something white lay on the ground that wasn't snow. LaFleur crouched to study it. The object in his palm turned out, when he examined it, to be a giant plaster toe. Suddenly, the mystery made sense. Jacques muttered every oath in his vocabulary of curses.

Behind him a crow cawed and clattered into flight. Startled, Jacques turned towards the sound. There, in the bushes, a giant figure loomed. Bigfoot had been watching, mocking him. LaFleur raised the rifle to his shoulder and fired, point-blank, at the giant form.

LaFleur edged closer to examine his handiwork, close enough to discover his target was two-dimensional, a mere cartoon. With a hole through the middle of his silly grin, a plywood moose advised Jacques to 'MAKE A FRIEND IN THE FOREST'.

Jacques kicked the figure over and stomped on it. As he did so, a small dog ran out of the forest and attacked his trouser leg. LaFleur aimed his rifle at the pest but couldn't get a clear shot that didn't have his own foot in it. He set his rifle aside and prised the wretched creature from his leg.

When Little Bob appeared and attacked his enemy, Harry decided it was time to intervene. Silently he slid down the tree trunk and dropped to the ground. The creature was too busy fighting Little Bob to see him. When he threw Little Bob into the air, Harry reached out and caught the dog. The male reached for his rifle. Harry slammed his foot down and felt the rifle break. The male felt for the small gun on his belt. Harry seized him by the trousers and hoisted him into the air. He dropped his pistol and cried out in pain.

A shot boomed, not far away. 'Harry!' George struggled towards the sound. Wrightwood clambered after him. The heavy, awkward castings made speed impossible. George tripped over a tree root and toppled. When he got up, he smashed his plaster feet against a tree. Wrightwood did the same. They ran.

Little Bob's frenzied barking guided them to a small clearing. The station wagon was parked there. Harry stood on its roof, while LaFleur lay unmoving beneath him. George ran towards them. 'Oh, no! Harry! Oh, God, no!'

Harry looked at George with a proud smile. While Harry wasn't looking, LaFleur slid off the car. He approached the family, begging, 'Help me. Please don't let it kill me.'

'Listen to me,' George said. 'Please. You're wrong. I was like you. I almost killed him. But it would have been murder. He's not an animal.'

Nancy said simply, 'He's our friend, Mr LaFleur.'

Doc said, 'For heaven's sake, Jock. Open your eyes!'

LaFleur said, 'You people are crazy. This is an animal. It could turn on you without warning.'

Without warning, all the excitement, the confusion and frustration of the past week boiled up inside George and exploded. He turned on the tracker. Seizing him by the shirt front, he slammed LaFleur into the car again and again. 'We won't let you harm him,' George yelled. 'You don't understand. We can't let you go!'

For a moment the rest of the family stared numbly at George. Harry looked shocked. 'George, stop!' Nancy pleaded. Then she turned to the Bigfoot. 'Harry, please?'

Harry sprang into action. He put one huge hand behind LaFleur's head to buffer it from bashing. With the other he pushed George away. Sternly he shook his head. No, George.

LaFleur was half mad with fear. 'Stop him! Don't let him kill me! Please! Stop him!'

Gently Harry stroked LaFleur's head, as he had seen Nancy do with Little Bob. LaFleur gazed into Harry's face. His voice grew quiet, almost meek. 'Please don't let him kill me.'

Harry snuggled LaFleur against his massive chest. Slowly the tracker relaxed in his embrace. His expression grew tranquil. Watching them, the family began to breathe more easily.

When LaFleur was calm, Harry released him. Backing away, LaFleur reached out a timid hand and touched Harry. He turned to the family. 'I'm so sorry. I had no idea. I feel like such a heel.'

• Chapter Forty-four

Jacques stood by while Wally Wrightwood took a picture of Bigfoot with his friends, the Hendersons. This was hardly how Jacques had expected Sasquatch to be shot. After the shutter clicked, the family portrait dissolved into a group hug.

'Well, Doc,' Jacques said. 'I guess it's over.'

'Over?' Wally said. 'Jocko, I haven't felt the old ticker thump like this in years. It's like going to heaven with your feet still on the ground.' Doc looked at Harry, then back at Jacques. 'And we get to share it with one of our oldest friends. What are you going to do, Jock?'

The fact is, Jacques had no idea what to do. His life's mission had just evaporated. Funny thing, though. It didn't really bother him. He shrugged and shot Doc something like a smile. 'Well, there's always Loch Ness.' He even liked it when Wally laughed.

Even more than he hated kissing, Ernie hated goodbyes. He could tell from the heavy, sort of damaged way he felt inside that this was really going to be one. Harry was going back to the forest. Before he went, Dad made a little speech. 'I guess this really is goodbye, Harry. I've never really got to thank you. You'll never know . . . of course you know what you've meant to us.'

Ernie could hear his Dad's voice crack. He was glad it wasn't him talking. He would have been bawling by now.

'You take care of yourself now, okay?' Dad said.

Harry reached out and pulled Dad up close. He patted him on the back. Then Harry said, 'Okay!'

Old Doc Wrightwood almost fell over. 'I can't believe it. They have a language!'

Dad nodded at Harry and Harry nodded back. With a smile, he turned towards the woods. Ernie moved close enough to put his arm around his dad. His mom put her arm around him. 'We're the luckiest people on the planet,' his dad whispered, in a voice that sounded all choked up. The whole family watched Harry walk away.

Except he didn't really walk away. He just went a little bit into the woods, and then something they thought was a tree moved up to him, and then another tree moved, and they were really Bigfeet, and Harry had a family. He led his wife and his kid back to meet the Hendersons. For a little bit the two families just stood there, staring at each other, with the dads out front. Then Harry started to walk towards Dad, and Dad walked towards Harry, and then, when they met in the middle, they hugged each other tight.

• Epilogue: And *Then* What Happened?

Well, what happened then is that everybody changed.

The biggest change was that Wally Wrightwood and Jacques LaFleur buried the hatchet and became friends. The Bigfoot mania brought so much business to Doc's museum that Jacques agreed to help him out for a while. He moved into the old caravan and eventually fixed it up so it was habitable. What the two old bachelors found was that they had more in common with each other than with anybody else. They enjoyed each other's company. They liked each other's cooking. They gave each other the courage to go to Grange Hall on Saturday night and dance with pretty widows. Both of them had been too single-minded, and too shy, to go before.

With the profits from the Bigfoot bonanza they built themselves a little cabin in the woods, close to the place they left off for Harry, near where the Hendersons built theirs. When things are slow at the store, they take to the woods. Harry and his family visit them. So do George and his.

Obsession dies hard, of course, but now the two old dream-chasers have a new cause. Having discovered that Bigfoot really does exist, they're fighting to have him added to the endangered-species list. Any day now, they expect a Congressional delegation to visit the Mount Rainier National Forest to meet Harry for themselves.

After her encounter with Harry and Jacques LaFleur, Irene Moffitt swore off junk food for good. She made Herb build her a greenhouse to protect her roses, took up exercise and gave up diets. She is now a fully licensed instructor of aquatic aerobics. Being busy, she no longer haunts the Hendersons' kitchen. When they get together for lunch or to play cards, George and Nancy are actually glad to see her.

The story of how George Henderson finessed his mid-life crisis and became a celebrated painter of Northwest wildlife is a little bit less simple. It didn't happen overnight.

First, Nancy got a part-time job for the Seattle Horticultural Society, tending the rare plants in the conservatory at Volunteer Park. That brought in enough money for George to go part-time at the sporting goods store. Yes, his father took him back. Despite his eccentricities, George was the best salesman he had.

The half days he spent at home, George painted. He painted like a man possessed.

His first one-man show, held at the Northwest Anthropological Institute and Bigfoot Museum, coincided with the publication of the last instalment of Jacques LaFleur's Bigfoot memoirs. It was a huge success. Every one of his paintings sold. Critics compared George's sensitive portraits of Bigfoot favourably with Albert Bierstadt's buffalo. He began to get commissions. The Washington State Arts Commission gave him a grant. George quit his job, this time for good. His father now takes an interest in his career.

The change in Sarah was dramatic. Her interest in Michael Jackson waned. She replaced posters of her former idol with wildlife posters. She got an after-school job at the office of the neighbourhood veterinarian to gain a little first-hand experience in her chosen field. She joined the Animal Protection League and got arrested picketing at the Animal Experimentation Laboratory at the University of Washington. While picketing, she met a high-school senior with similar interests and began her first real relationship with a member of the opposite sex. The Hendersons were proud to bail their daughter out of the city jail.

And Ernie? Well, boys will be boys. He's still in the fifth grade. He still plays baseball. He still torments his older sister. He still sleeps with Max, the teddy bear. He's still fiercely proud of his father. He proved it by getting a black eye in a fight with Frankie MacDowell because Frankie said something about artists being wimps and Ernie insisted that he take it back. Ernie won the fight. Frankie went home with two black eyes and a fat lip. His dad got mad at him for fighting.

Ernie's very favourite things of all are the vacations when the family pack up their new mini-van and head for the forest to visit their friends Doc and Jacques and Harry. The last time they stayed for three weeks. Ernie taught Harry how to say 'awesome'. Harry taught Ernie how to catch fish with his hands. Doc and Jacques have invited Ernie to spend all of next summer in the woods with them. Ernie is already trying to get his parents to agree. In part, he does this by being annoying around the house.

Harry is known among his kind as 'the One Who Left the Forest'. He is glad to have gone and glad to be back home. Now he has the best of both worlds. Except perhaps for eating, there is nothing Harry enjoys more than watching his mate and his friend's mate gather flowers in the meadows, or his son and his friend's son running together through the woods, or, of an evening, sitting with his friend beside the lake.

Other Books from Puffin

THE PRIME MINISTER'S BRAIN

Gillian Cross

The fiendish DEMON HEADMASTER plans to gain control of No. 10 Downing Street and lure the Prime Minister into his evil clutches.

JASON BODGER AND THE PRIORY GHOST

Gene Kemp

A ghost story, both funny and exciting, about Jason, the bane of every teacher's life, who is pursued by the ghost of a little nun from the twelfth century!

HALFWAY ACROSS THE GALAXY AND TURN LEFT

Robin Klein

A humorous account of what happens to a family banished from their planet Zygron, when they have to spend a period of exile on Earth.

SUPER GRAN TO THE RESCUE

Forrest Wilson

The punchpacking, baddiebiffing escapades of the world's No. 1 senior citizen superhero – Super Gran! Now a devastating series on ITV!

TOM TIDDLER'S GROUND

John Rowe Townsend

Vic and Brain are given an old rowing boat which leads to the unravelling of a mystery and a happy reunion of two friends. An exciting adventure story.

COME BACK SOON

Judy Gardiner

Val's family seem quite an odd bunch and their life is hectic but happy. But then Val's mother walks out on them and Val's carefree life is suddenly quite different. This is a moving but funny story.

AMY'S EYES

Richard Kennedy

When a doll changes into a man it means that anything might happen . . . and in this magical story all kinds of strange and wonderful things do happen to Amy and her sailor doll, the Captain. Together they set off on a fantastic journey on a quest for treasure more valuable than mere gold.

ASTERCOTE

Penelope Lively

Astercote village was destroyed by plague in the fourteenth century and Mair and her brother Peter find themselves caught up in a strange adventure when an ancient superstition is resurrected.

THE HOUNDS OF THE MÓRRÍGAN

Pat O'Shea

When the Great Queen Mórrígan, evil creature from the world of Irish mythology, returns to destroy the world, Pidge and Brigit are the children chosen to thwart her. How they go about it makes an hilarious, moving story, full of totally original and unforgettable characters.